MAX

The DETECTIVE CAT

The CATNAP CAPER

illustrated by
NICOLA KINNEAR

Sarah Todd Taylor

nosy
crow

First published 2019 by Nosy Crow Ltd
The Crow's Nest, 14 Baden Place, Crosby Row
London SE1 1YW
www.nosycrow.com

ISBN: 978 1 78800 065 9

Nosy Crow and associated logos are trademarks
and/or registered trademarks of Nosy Crow Ltd

A CIP catalogue record for this book will be available from the British Library

Printed and bound in Great Britain by Clays Ltd, Elcograf S.p.A

Papers used by Nosy Crow are made from wood grown in
sustainable forests.

1 3 5 7 9 10 8 6 4 2

For Seren

S. T.

For Paul

N.K.

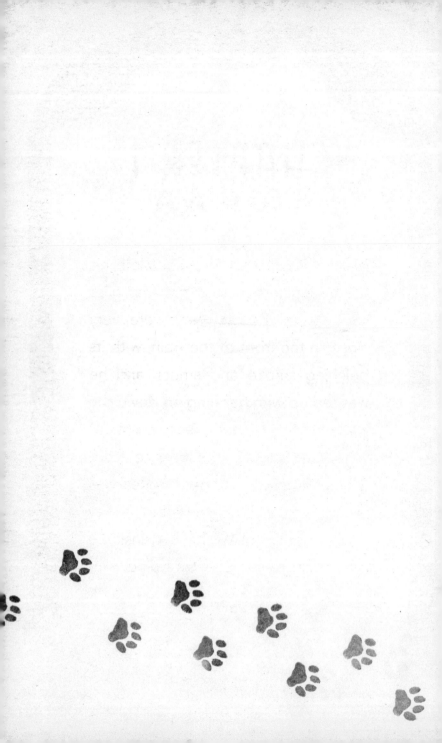

CHAPTER 1
A Cat in Paris

Maximilian flicked the soot off his tail and glared across the first-class carriage at Agnes. They were very close to the front of the train, with its belching smoke and smuts, and he was fed up with her flinging down the window every five minutes to point out everything she could see while filling the carriage with smoke. Agnes was always like this. On their visit to Fawley Castle last October she had insisted on freezing everyone by riding with the car window down so that she could catch a glimpse of the castle before anyone else.

"Stop jiggling around like that," Sylvia snapped as Agnes jumped up for the hundredth time to squeal with delight at yet another cow. Maximilian swiped a shower of soot from his nose and miaowed in annoyance. They were on their way to one of the most elegant cities in the world and he was determined to make a good impression, which would be very difficult if his fur looked grubby. He tucked his tail around himself and set to work grooming it to perfection.

"I want to see Paris," Agnes sulked. "We've come all this way and all you can do is read your silly book!"

She collapsed on the seat next to Maximilian and tickled him on the top of his head.

"I bet *you're* excited, aren't you, Max," she said. "You'll be seeing Madame Emerald again, and we all know how fond you are of her."

"And she's Max's biggest fan. Isn't she, Max?" Sylvia said.

Maximilian smiled. He *was* looking forward to seeing Madame again. It was almost a year since he had foiled a plot by a dastardly jewel thief to kidnap Madame and impersonate her at the Theatre Royal, where he lived. That had been Maximilian's first case, and now Madame had rewarded him and his theatre friends with a trip to France, where she was one of the judges at the most prestigious singing competition in Europe – "The Voice of Paris". Madame Emerald was elegant and brave and exquisitely talented. It would be wonderful to be in her company again.

Across the carriage, Maximilian's best friend, Oscar, smiled at him from the seat next to Sylvia. Unlike Maximilian, who was curled up in a relaxed ball, Oscar sat upright, his paws resting lightly on the edge of the wooden seat, as if ready to spring to the ground at a moment's notice. Oscar had resisted all of Sylvia's attempts to encourage him to have a catnap and Maximilian wondered whether he might be more comfortable on the train's roof. Oscar lived on the roof of the Theatre Royal and never enjoyed being trapped indoors, even in a train carriage.

"Do you think we'll be able to go *shopping*?" Agnes breathed, her eyes gleaming at the magic of the word.

Agnes and Sylvia were the two most talented members of the Theatre Royal's chorus. It was, according to Agnes, "the best job in the whole world," but they were not yet grand stars who could afford diamonds, chocolates and taxis. Maximilian knew that Agnes and Sylvia had little spare money after paying for their rather shabby rooms overlooking one of London's less illustrious streets, but they loved to do what Agnes called "window-shopping". This meant putting on their best coats and hats and walking along Bond Street looking at all the fine things in the windows and imagining what life would be like if they could afford even *one* of the splendid outfits they picked out in their minds.

"I hear that Paris has the most wonderful shops in the whole world," Agnes continued. "It has chocolate shops crammed with caramels and truffles in every flavour you can think of, and clothes shops just brimming with silks and satins..."

Maximilian saw Sylvia shoot a wistful look at her book, but it was hopeless. Agnes was in full flow and did not stop until the train chugged into Gare du Nord station, pulling up at a crowded platform packed with smartly dressed travellers. Maximilian peered out of the window, careful not to let his nose press against it in case of dust. Across the platform a great green engine was being coaxed into life by two grimy-looking men in overalls shovelling coal into a spitting firebox. The air was thick with noise as passengers hurried to find their coaches, and porters dashed to and fro, pushing rattling cages crammed with luggage. Somewhere in the distance a shrill whistle blew and, with a combination of chugs and creaks, an engine began to pull out of the station, sending clouds of smoke up towards the glass roof.

Agnes dashed to the door that led into the corridor running the length of the train and threw it open. There was a cry of alarm as it narrowly avoided knocking over an elderly woman in an elaborately-brimmed hat. The woman glared at Agnes and whisked her gloved hand at a nervous looking boy in a blue and cream uniform who was staggering under a pile of suitcases. Agnes muttered an embarrassed "sorry" and stepped out into the corridor, where she was instantly enveloped in green velvet.

"My *darlings!*" cried a familiar voice, light and musical, and the beautiful face of Madame Emerald appeared at the door, her arms wrapped around Agnes. She was wearing a cloak embroidered with silver swirls and seed pearls, and the soft curls of her dark hair peeped out from under a close-fitted felt hat trimmed with silk roses.

Maximilian sprang to the floor and miaowed his "we are overjoyed to be here and it is an honour to see you again" miaow. It was the longest and most melodic of his miaows and he had been practising it carefully, adding a celebratory whisk of his tail, so it was most irritating to have it ruined by Sylvia of all people. Not caring that he was in the middle of an elegant greeting, Sylvia threw herself at Madame Emerald and drowned him out with a cacophony of "thank you"s. Maximilian gave a little "I was talking actually" cough, but Madame Emerald, Sylvia and Agnes were too busy to notice him.

It was only after Sylvia had said for the fiftieth time how excited they were to be in Paris, and Agnes had extracted a list of all the best shopping streets, and Madame had found out which carriage Monsieur Lavroche and Mrs Garland were in (the two of them having wisely decided not to travel in the same carriage as Agnes) that Madame finally disentangled herself from the two girls and looked at Maximilian.

"There he is!" she said, her lovely face beaming down on him. "My daring rescuer. How has Max been?"

"He's solved another mystery," Sylvia said proudly, referring to the events before Christmas when Maximilian and Oscar had prevented the Fawley family jewels from falling into the hands of a most audacious criminal.

Maximilian miaowed his "may I present my good friend, Oscar" miaow and Oscar padded over to execute a charming bow. Madame Emerald clapped a hand to her chest.

"You darling! Oh, it is so wonderful to have you all with me again!" she cried. "What an adventure we are going to have!"

CHAPTER 2
The Voice of Paris

"I'm going to have the *pain au chocolat*," declared Agnes, putting on an air of sophisticated elegance and trying out her best French accent.

The waiter, his face one of bland politeness, took away the plate bearing the crumbs from Agnes' five croissants and placed another silver coffee pot in the middle of the table.

They were sat having a very late breakfast in a tiny café that looked out on to one of Paris's gardens. Their waiter had raised an eyebrow on discovering that two of the seats at the table booked for five were meant for cats, but he had shown them to a charming spot and the cutlery and water glasses at Maximilian and Oscar's places had been discreetly removed and replaced with two shallow dishes of cream. Nothing, it seemed, was too much trouble if it was for Madame Emerald. She had found them the finest suites in the best hotel in the city and had come to fetch them the next morning for as many pastries as they wanted while Monsieur Lavroche visited friends and Mrs Garland explored the city.

"Tell us all about the competition," Sylvia said, smiling thanks at the waiter as he delivered a plate piled high with *pains au chocolat* to the table.

Madame Emerald settled back in her chair and folded her napkin on to her plate.

"My sweets, it's been such a month," she

said. "We've had concert after concert, some most thrilling, some very dreary, and now we're down to the final four singers."

"And what are they like?" Agnes asked.

Madame sighed. "Divine, each and every one of them. That's what makes it so difficult." She looked at Maximilian and Oscar.

"Who would you choose, Max? There's Albert, a really *wonderful* bass. Such deep tones and a very good, amiable man. Then there's Julienne; she's the most divine soprano, though she'd better make the most of her career before Agnes here catches up with her and nabs all the good roles."

Maximilian glanced over at Agnes, who had gone a very bright pink. Agnes had a beautiful voice and Maximilian was sure that she had a glittering career ahead of her.

"Henri is a little precious about things," continued Madame Emerald, "but he has some lovely top notes and can sing love songs with more feeling than anyone I've ever met. Then there's Minette."

She paused and peered over at the counter where a sweet-faced girl with auburn bobbed hair was counting up a customer's bill. The customer barely made eye contact with her as he handed over several notes in payment and left with his change. Maximilian saw her eyes flick to the tip jar on the counter and just for a second her lovely smile flickered a little.

"Minette," Madame Emerald called, raising her hand in greeting.

The girl beamed at Madame Emerald and, slipping out from behind the counter, joined them at the table.

"Yes, Madame?" she said. "Is there anything more we can get for you?"

Maximilian looked over at Oscar. "What a voice!" he miaowed. Oscar nodded. Minette's voice was low and lilting, like the melody of a calling dove. Maximilian and Oscar often disagreed over voices. Maximilian adored the high tones of Madame and Agnes, whereas Oscar, though admitting that they were skilled, preferred the lower tones of the voices called *mezzo-soprano*. "They may be less flashy," he would say, "but they are often far superior."

They were united in their admiration of Minette's voice, though, and liked her even more when she whisked a jug of cream from the tray of a passing waiter and generously topped up the dishes in front of them.

"Minette, these are my friends from London," Madame said, introducing them all. "Minette is our final contestant. You will hear her at our concert this evening."

Sylvia and Agnes gushed enthusiastically about how much they were looking forward to hearing everyone sing. Maximilian miaowed his "it will be a delight to be at such an illustrious event" miaow and Oscar inclined his head in a very handsome bow.

Minette, blushing a little at all the attention, said that she must get back to the counter and was about to leave when the door of the café burst open and Mrs Garland fell through, her arms overflowing with bags and parcels. Barely able to see over the top of them, she shimmied her way between the tables and headed for where they were all seated.

"Oh, you saved me a chair. How lovely of you," she blustered, not seeing Maximilian, and, before Sylvia could warn her, she dropped her pile of parcels all over him. Maximilian cried out in alarm as a hail of buttons and bags and ribbons poured down, leaving him smothered under a mountain of brown paper and twine.

"Oh, Max!" cried Sylvia, stifling a giggle.

Maximilian shook his head with annoyance and a bundle of ribbons fell out of a bag and garlanded his ears like a multicoloured wig. He let out a miaow of irritation and Sylvia could

bear it no more. She screamed with laughter and covered her face with her hands. Agnes joined in and even Madame Emerald smiled rather wryly at him. It was most undignified.

"Oh, I'm so sorry, Max," Mrs Garland gasped, snatching the ribbons from his head and gathering the parcels up into her arms. A passing waiter provided a chair for her without a word, as well as a small table for her things. "I've found the most wonderful haberdasheries. Sylvia, your dress for next season's winter show will have this on it." She dug through one of the bags and produced a piece of lace so fine that Maximilian had to squint to see it. Sylvia peered at it doubtfully.

"Will the audience be able to see that?" she said.

"Ah," said Mrs Garland. "Watch this."

She held the lace up to the morning sun streaming through the window. It seemed to explode in a myriad of rainbows, shimmering with light and colour. Sylvia's eyes widened and Maximilian could see that Agnes was looking a little envious that she would be getting a costume made from such finery. Mrs Garland had plenty for everyone, though, and after she'd packed the lace away, they spent a happy half-hour rooting through her purchases, discussing how beautiful the company would look once Mrs Garland got to work on it all with her needle and thread.

"Let's go for a walk," Madame Emerald said eventually, looking at her watch. "We have a few hours before I need to be back at the concert hall and there are so many sights that I want to show you all."

They packed up and paid their bill, wishing Minette good day. Maximilian noticed that Madame left a very generous tip as they made their way to the door. Madame had just taken hold of the handle when the door flew open once more and a small, round woman wrapped in a brightly coloured shawl almost collided with her. Ignoring them entirely, the woman looked wildly around the room. She dashed to a table where an elderly woman was reading the morning paper, where she collapsed into a chair and burst into tears.

As Max was shepherded out of the café by Agnes, he heard the woman blurt out one word through her sobs.

"Kidnapped!"

CHAPTER 3
The Four Singers

"Kidnapped?" asked Oscar. "Are you sure?"

They were sat on the roof of the Opéra Musique, the grand concert hall where "The Voice of Paris" competition would be held. It was the most beautiful concert venue in all of Paris: a perfect circle of green and gold. Four tiers of plush velvet seats of exquisite sea green rose high up to the painted ceiling, from which hung a chandelier shaped like a vast sunburst suspended in mid-air. From the wooden panelling that ran round the balconies to the ornate plasterwork that covered the ceiling and cascaded down the walls, everything was covered in gold.

The roof, of course, was as plain and dusty as any old rooftop in London, and Oscar had made a beeline for it, saying that he felt far more at home there than in all the finery below.

"She definitely said kidnapped," said Maximilian. "And did you see how upset she looked?" His tail tingled, the way it always did when he could sense that a mystery was nearby. What a pity he had been whisked out of the café. It was irritatingly bad timing, when there was the possibility of another case at his paw tips.

Oscar sighed. "Well, we're unlikely to see her again," he mused. "I suppose this one will have to be solved by the police."

Maximilian frowned. It would be rather splendid to solve a kidnapping. Though

Maximilian did not like to admit it, one of his favourite things about the cases he had solved had been how much of a fuss everyone made of him afterwards, and a kidnapping would make him a real hero. It was true that he had rescued Madame Emerald from a team of kidnappers, but he hadn't actually *known* that she had been kidnapped, so he wasn't sure that counted.

Oscar looked at him wryly. "It's no good sulking about it," he said, causing Maximilian to frown even more, because no one likes to be caught sulking.

"I think I will go and see what they are up to downstairs," he said with great dignity and, sticking his tail in the air to show he was *not* sulky and was *certainly not* storming out, he left Oscar on the roof and headed for the dressing rooms.

He found Sylvia and Agnes gathered in the

suite of rooms that had been reserved for Madame Emerald. Madame and Sylvia were lounging on a huge sofa while Agnes riffled through a rail of dresses, exclaiming with delight over each one and teasing out the skirts to hold against herself.

"They're insisting that each of the judges has a different outfit for every night of the competition," Madame Emerald was saying. "Can you imagine the extravagance?"

Maximilian padded into the room and sprang up to a particularly comfortable-looking chair. The cushion sighed as he sank into it, enveloping him in softness. In the Opéra Musique even the dressing rooms were opulent, with plush seating and carpets and beautifully carved dressing tables accentuated with gold lacquer work. Madame's dressing table was covered with bouquets of flowers and chocolate boxes in pastel shades tied up with silk ribbons. Maximilian thoroughly approved of all this splendour. He draped his wonderful tail over the arm of the chair, glad to see how beautiful it looked against the dark red of the fabric.

He was just settling back for a short catnap when Minette walked past the dressing room. A deep-green dress was draped over her arm and she waved happily at Sylvia and Agnes as she passed.

"Is that your gown for this evening, Minette?" Madame Emerald called.

Minette paused and came into the room, shaking out the dress in front of her. It was a simple gown of green chiffon with a delicate frill at the shoulder and a fluted hem. Maximilian could see that it would look extremely pretty on her, but it was very plain compared with the magnificent gowns that hung on Madame's rails.

"I found it in a market in town," Minette said, her cheeks pink with excitement. "Isn't it lovely? It only had a tiny tear next to the buttons, but I managed to fix it and it's a perfect fit." The words came out in a rush and Minette paused and looked down at the floor.

Maximilian began to suspect that Minette did not have much money. She had looked very longingly at the tips jar in the café and now here she was performing in Paris's most illustrious singing competition in a hand-me-down gown.

Madame rose to her feet and put a hand on Minette's arm. "You will look utterly charming, my dear," she said kindly. Minette lifted her chin and smiled. She opened her mouth to thank Madame when a tall, dark-haired woman appeared at the door, dressed from top to toe in sequins. Her frock was midnight blue, cut strikingly low down the front. At her throat was a double strand of diamonds.

"Henri has been looking for you, Madame. I think he wishes to check that his choice of

26

music is acceptable," she said. Maximilian saw Minette take in the other woman's gown and move to hide her own. All the excitement had drained from her face. Maximilian tried to miaow his "I think you will look lovely" miaow, but found that he had sunk so far into the cushion that it was rather difficult to lift his head up. All that came out was a rather garbled "mrowl" that made Sylvia look at him in alarm. Really, he was not managing to look his best on

this trip, and in such elegant surroundings as well!

He decided to go and explore the side of the stage. It was one of his favourite places in the Theatre Royal back in London. He would perch on the stage manager's table and watch as the talented crew turned the theatre's stage into a night-time woodland or a haunted castle or even the depths of the sea. He had lived at the Theatre Royal for over a year now, but it still seemed magical to him. The wings of the Opéra Musique were bigger than the Theatre Royal's, but instead of being crammed to bursting with set and props they held only four tables. On three of them was a water bottle and a glass. The fourth held several bottles, a huge woollen muffler and a silver frame with a picture of a handsome and beaming young man holding a large glass trophy. Maximilian jumped on to the table to investigate, but there were no clues as to who the young man in the photo was. He peered at the trophy, but it was no use. Maximilian, unlike Oscar, had never learned to read.

"Get down off there!" snapped a voice behind him. Maximilian wheeled round and came face to face with the young man in the photo. He had a very smooth face and, if he had been a cat, Maximilian would have sworn that he spent a good part of his day grooming that lustrous hair of his. It lay perfectly flat and shining against his head, not a hair out of place.

Maximilian leapt to the floor, slightly embarrassed at having been caught snooping. Today was just one embarrassment after another. The young man aimed a sly kick at him and swept to the table, where he checked everything, muttering in a high, whining voice about "disgusting cat hairs".

"Ah, the famous Max," said a deep, booming voice and a jovial-looking man with an enormous chest and at least four chins breezed into the wings. "Minette has been telling me all about you." He folded himself over and pressed his face up to Maximilian's. "Splendid," he boomed. "Marvellous to have a cat around the place."

"I disagree, Albert. Think of the fur, think of the mess," said the woman in the sequins, coming up behind the man named Albert. She pronounced it "Al-bear", which Maximilian assumed was the French fashion, though he was sure that Bert, the Theatre Royal's stage manager, would declare it "silly and fancy, and what's wrong with plain old Bert?"

Minette was the last to enter the wings. She had changed into her frock and, as Maximilian had thought, it looked delightful on her, the green a perfect colour for her auburn hair. He looked from Henri to Albert to Julienne to Minette. So these were the final contestants in "The Voice of Paris" competition. The four singers. Maximilian already knew which one he wanted to win.

CHAPTER 4
The Grey Cat

Maximilian perched on the edge of the orchestra pit, watching the auditorium fill with excited concertgoers. The stalls and lower galleries sparkled with the beads of the ladies' gowns and the jewels in their chic hairstyles. Up in the very highest circle, where the concert hall sold its cheaper seats, shop workers still in their crisp uniforms and women wrapped in woollen shawls craned their heads to see if they could spy anyone famous below. In front of the stage, just behind the conductor's podium, was a small platform with three seats for the judges. A rather pinched-faced man in a very neatly fitted evening coat with a gardenia in his buttonhole was seated in one of them, leafing through a musical score and wrinkling his nose. From time to time he marked something in the score with a slim, crystal-topped pencil. After a few minutes, Madame Emerald joined him, dressed in a beautiful gown of pink silk. Maximilian waved his tail at her in greeting. He had spent a full half-hour on it and he was sure that it looked perfect. So long as no one covered him in soot or ribbons or smothered him with cushions, he was sure that he could show Paris what an elegant, sophisticated and modern cat looked like. Madame Emerald waved back at him, but the pinched-faced man's nose creased with disgust and he turned to Madame and said something that made her frown.

If the judges were taking their places, then

the concert would be starting soon. Maximilian sprang to the stage and nudged the curtain back with his paw, ready to take his place backstage. He took one final glance behind him at the concert hall, waiting for the magical expectant hush that always fell just before curtain up, and that is when he saw the woman from the café.

She was seated in a box near the edge of the stage with three companions, all of whom were crowded round her, handing her handkerchiefs and shaking their heads at one another in sympathy. The woman had a beaded shawl wrapped tightly around her and her eyes were puffy and red. Maximilian remembered the word she had uttered to her friend as she collapsed into a chair at the café, and he felt his tail tingle. He was vaguely aware of the final judge taking their seat, the conductor appearing at the side of the stage in a spotlight, the dimming of the lights and the hush of the audience, but he paid all this no attention. Instead he leapt to the floor and made his way out of the auditorium, towards the stairs that would lead to the dress circle.

Maximilian slipped into the box and tucked himself in the shadows at the back where he would not be seen. The concert had begun and a high soprano voice was filling the hall, the notes sparking in the air. *It must be Julienne*, thought Maximilian. He was rather disappointed to find that she was exceptionally talented, with a voice that could change in an instant from light trills that sent the notes bouncing round the hall to beautiful long phrases that swooped through the air. She held the whole audience spellbound.

The whole audience, that is, except for the woman from the café. Ignoring her friends, who seemed now to be trying to listen to the concert and whose glances to one another were notably less sympathetic than before, the woman was engrossed in a photograph that she held in trembling hands.

"This was taken only the other day," the woman sobbed. "Look at how beautiful she is."

The woman on her right rolled her eyes and put down the opera glasses she had been using to get a closer look at Julienne's dress.

"I'm sure she'll turn up, Monique," she muttered. "Leave it to the police."

The woman called Monique shook her head and let out another sob. "The police just said that it was the eleventh this month and they had more important things to worry about. Imagine! Eleven beautiful darlings kidnapped, and no one seems to care." At this she burst into floods of tears and buried her face in her hands.

A woman in a rather drab mushroom frock took the photograph and passed her another handkerchief. "And you've no idea how they got her?" she asked.

"I went in to give her breakfast this morning and she was gone!" Monique wailed. "And it was her favourite. Salmon with cream. Oh, my poor baby girl!"

Maximilian frowned. It was clear that they were talking about a child, but salmon with cream sounded like a most peculiar breakfast for an infant. He ventured out of the shadows to try to get a look at the picture, but the woman in the mushroom dress was holding it in front of her. Only when she passed it back to Monique did he catch a glimpse of it. It was a photograph of a large cushion, plump and tasselled. On the cushion, alert and bright-eyed, staring into the camera for her portrait, was a sleek grey cat with a collar of square-cut diamonds.

Maximilian felt his fur standing on end. He dashed out of the box and headed towards the stage, his mind a whirl. A *catnapper* was at large. Eleven cats had already been taken, and from the sound of it the police had no interest in investigating. It would be up to Maximilian to save them. As he dashed through the door that led backstage he heard the audience erupt into applause. Julienne must have finished her programme. Maximilian reached the side of the stage to find Oscar sat waiting for him.

"I came to apologise," the black cat said. "I'm sorry I said you were sulking. You've missed Julienne. She was magnificent."

"Never mind that," gasped Maximilian, and quickly filled him in on everything he had learned in the box.

Maximilian and Oscar discussed the case all through the concert. While Henri sang cloying love songs they debated whether the cats had really been kidnapped or had simply wandered off. While Albert performed booming pieces about warrior gods they pondered how difficult it would be to kidnap a clever cat. Dogs, of course, were far less intelligent, which would make them easier to take, but a kidnapper would need to work hard to fool a cat.

Then Minette took to the stage and they stopped discussing the case altogether.

Minette stood in the middle of the stage in her simple green chiffon and wove a spell into the air around her. A beautiful low note hung in the air, pure and still, before climbing higher and turning into a wonderful run of staccato notes that swept downwards again to the captivated audience.

At the end of Minette's programme of three songs there was a moment of silence as the audience took a deep breath and sighed as one. Then the whole concert hall broke into thunderous applause.

"We had better wait in Madame's room for Sylvia and Agnes," said Maximilian as the curtain swept across the stage.

They made their way up to the corridor where the dressing rooms were, past the room where Albert was reading the newspaper with his feet on his dressing table, past Julienne entertaining a group of friends and drinking champagne, past Henri smoothing yet more oil over his hair. As they rounded a corner near Madame Emerald's room Maximilian saw a large woman in a voluminous black evening gown and beaded shawl walking away down the corridor.

Over her shoulder peeped the head of a grey cat with a collar of square-cut diamonds.

CHAPTER 5
The Most Unfortunate Misunderstanding

Maximilian sprang into action at once. With a cry of "Stop! Kidnap!" he dashed down the corridor. When he was a few cat-lengths away from the woman he leapt up and landed on her shoulder next to the grey cat. The woman shrieked and batted at Maximilian with one hand, clutching the grey cat with the other.

"I'm here to save you!" Maximilian hissed at the grey cat, hoping that French cats spoke Cat the same way that English cats did. "Wriggle free if you can."

The grey cat looked more frightened of Maximilian than of its kidnapper and took a great swipe at Maximilian's nose with its claws. The woman cried out again, then Maximilian heard Madame Emerald's voice.

"Max! What on earth are you doing to Madame Belfourte?"

Madame Emerald, her face clouded with confusion, had arrived at the end of the corridor, together with the pinched-faced judge.

Maximilian hung from the woman's shoulder, his claws snagging on her gauzy dress. He could feel a trickle of blood running down his nose and caking in his beautiful fur. Madame Emerald was staring at him with a look that most certainly did not say "what a heroic rescue you have achieved." He began to feel rather foolish and, with a little miaow that was meant to say "clearly there has been a mistake and you are probably not a dastardly kidnapper", he let go of the lady's shoulder and dropped to the ground.

Madame Emerald hurried over and examined Madame Belfourte's dress.

"Nothing torn, thank goodness, but I'm afraid your dressmaker will have to reset some of the beading. Honestly, Max, what on earth were you thinking?"

Maximilian looked at the ground. Nothing had gone right since he had arrived in Paris, and he had *so* wanted to appear suave and sophisticated. Oscar, he noted, was suddenly conveniently absent.

"I thought he was a kidnapper," said Madame Belfourte. "There have been the most awful cases of kidnapping of beautiful cats like dear Peppi, you know; ten this month." She had clearly not heard of the latest cat to go missing.

"Far too much fuss about nothing," said

the male judge. "It's only cats, after all. Nasty creatures, leaving their fur everywhere. Paris's houses will be better off without them."

Max felt his hackles rising. He opened his mouth to give out his "cats are the noblest creatures in the world" miaow, but Madame Belfourte beat him to it.

"How could you say such a thing, Pierre!" she cried. "My Peppi is the most precious thing in my life. I think he should come into the dressing room with us. I don't like to let him out of my sight with that terrible villain on the loose."

"Oh, Peppi will be quite safe with Max," said Madame Emerald. "He saved *me* from a kidnapper in London, you know. He's quite the detective on the quiet, when he's not attacking my friends." She looked sternly at Maximilian, but Madame Belfourte's attitude to him had changed entirely. Setting the grey cat on the ground, she swept an alarmed Maximilian up into her arms and planted a huge kiss on his cheek.

"Never mind, you gorgeous thing. I'm sure you meant well," she laughed. She let him down to the ground again and took Madame Emerald's arm.

"Shall we leave them to get acquainted while we discuss our scores for this evening's concert?" she asked, herding the other two judges into the dressing room. As she closed the door, Maximilian heard the pinched-faced man say, "Julienne was exquisite as always. Quality will always show and she is from a very distinguished family…"

The grey cat eyed Maximilian dubiously. Maximilian was feeling utterly wretched. How embarrassing it all was. He was very glad when Oscar padded up to them and introduced himself. Oscar never put anything like as much effort into his appearance as Maximilian did, and he spent half his life on the dusty roof of

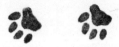

the Theatre Royal, sleeping out in all weathers, but in spite of all this he was a gentleman from his whiskers to his paws and Maximilian marvelled at how he accomplished it.

"My name is Peppi," said the grey cat. "Madame Belfourte is one of the most respected ladies of music in Paris. She holds at least two concerts a month in her house by the Eiffel Tower, and anyone who is *anyone* in the city's music scene has played on her wonderful pianoforte."

"And what is she doing here?" asked Oscar politely.

Peppi straightened his collar with one paw. "Judging, of course. Madame Belfourte is the premier judge of "The Voice of Paris". It's the most prestigious role in the competition. The premier judge is always invited to the best parties." Maximilian blushed. How simply awful to have attacked one of the judges! What must Madame Emerald think of him?

"The other judge is Pierre," went on Peppi, thankfully oblivious to Maximilian's mortification. "Everyone expected him to be premier judge this year, but at the last minute the organisers invited Madame Belfourte. Pierre is furious, which is rather delicious, given his horrible views on cats."

Maximilian remembered the way the man's face had twisted with disgust and shuddered. Much as he loved a puzzle, people who did not appreciate cats were utterly unfathomable.

"They'll be in there for ages," Peppi said, grooming a little dust off his paw. "Pierre will want Julienne to win, but judges' deliberations take at least an hour and they all need to agree who is progressing best and who will sing first tomorrow. It's *terribly* important."

"While they are all busy," Oscar said, "why don't we explore? I expect Monsieur Peppi knows all about this beautiful city."

In spite of Oscar's flattery, Peppi looked a

little uncertain. "Madame Bellourte doesn't like me to wander too far," he said. "She worries."

"We can be back before she even knows we're gone," Oscar promised.

🐾

But Oscar had not reckoned on a cat like Peppi, thought Maximilian, as they paused for the fifteenth time at the top of a tilting roof while Peppi crouched low, his claws gripping the slates, every muscle tensed.

"We won't see much at this rate," Maximilian remarked to Oscar. They had only crossed four rooftops and Peppi had had to be coaxed across every jump. Paris was wonderful from the rooftops. The lights of the city stretched out for miles and below them they could hear violins playing and smell the mouth-watering aroma of steak cooking in tiny bistros packed to bursting with people. Waiters in long white aprons dashed to and fro carrying six plates at once or balancing huge carafes on silver trays. It all reminded Maximilian that it was a long time since he had had any supper and he was worried that they would have to go back to the concert hall before he caught even a glimpse of the famous Eiffel Tower.

"I seem to remember a certain cat being the same only a year ago," Oscar said, looking meaningfully at Maximilian. "You need to be more patient with our host, my friend."

Maximilian looked back at Peppi and felt a little guilty. That first night crossing the skyline of London he had been just as terrified as Peppi was now, marvelling at how deftly Oscar could dash across the rooftops and jump from gable to gable, turning in mid-air. He determined to be a little kinder.

"I'm sorry for the misunderstanding earlier," he said to Peppi, who was teetering across the slates. "There was a lady in the concert hall whose cat was kidnapped only today, and they looked exactly like you. I saw the photo."

Peppi opened his mouth to say something and his back paw slipped a little. He let out a "mrowl" of alarm and squeezed his eyes tight shut. Clearly he was not a cat who could concentrate on two things at once. Maximilian waited till he had crossed safely before he began again.

"Grey with a diamante collar," he said. "Really, quite like you."

Peppi frowned. "That sounds like Winter Star," he said. "She is a really beautiful cat. I'm not surprised you thought she was me." Maximilian was about to suggest that this was a little conceited, but he caught Oscar's warning look and thought better of it.

"She lives over there," Peppi said, pointing a paw towards a cream townhouse with tall, narrow windows and window boxes overflowing with flowers. A long balcony of intricately wrought ironwork ran the length of the top floor.

"If someone could get on to the roof they could drop down to the balcony and get in that way," mused Maximilian, feeling his tail tingle the way it always did when he was solving a puzzle.

Peppi ignored him and pointed to another house a few streets away. "That was the scene of the first kidnapping," he said. "That one with the wide bay windows. The entire household was away having dinner on the river and when they returned, their new kitten, Mathilde, had been taken from her basket."

"How awful," said Oscar.

"Was Mathilde grey as well?" asked Maximilian, spotting a possible link, but Peppi shook his head. "A really lovely tabby with such striking black and cinnamon markings. There was a picture of her in the *Gazette*, in her basket, surrounded by roses. Her owner is an artist."

Maximilian thought that roses and art was rather getting away from the point, but Peppi clasped his front paws together and sighed, utterly forgetting all thoughts of how high they were and how treacherous his footing was.

"Speaking of photographs, you must come and visit me the day after tomorrow," he said. "I'm going to have my photograph taken by Zelie." From the excitement with which he said this it was clear that Maximilian and Oscar were meant to know who Zelie was.

"She's the most exciting young photographer in the city!" Peppi exclaimed. "Very chic and most exclusive. She only photographs the most elegant clients, and there is a tremendously long waiting list for a sitting with her. Oh, do say you'll come."

Maximilian was not sure that he wanted to sit watching Peppi preen and pose all afternoon. He was beginning to think that the grey cat was a little fussy. On the other paw, it would be most impolite to turn down an invitation and, after everything that had happened that day, Maximilian was anxious to show that he knew how to behave in polite society.

"It's easy to find our little house," Peppi said. "Just head for the Eiffel Tower, and when you come to a park with a carousel in the middle, we are the pink house that overlooks the lake of swans. It's quite a tiny apartment: I hope you won't find it too crowded a place to spend the afternoon."

Maximilian was about to say that it would be a pleasure to visit when a clocktower bell broke through the bustle of the streets below, chiming half past the hour. Peppi suddenly looked panic-stricken and turned to look over the rooftops at the concert hall.

"Madame will be frantic if we're late back!" he said. "It was quarter to when the curtain came down. We've been ever so long."

And, not thinking of how frightened he had been earlier, he dashed across to the edge and took a great leap to the rooftop opposite.

CHAPTER 6
Tea With Madame Elise

The next day there was no concert to prepare for, so Madame Emerald arrived at the hotel very early and carried Sylvia and Agnes away in a gleaming bottle-green car. Maximilian curled up on Madame's lap. Oscar perched neatly at her side, his chin lifted high in a most gentlemanly manner. They sped down avenues lined with trees of falling pink blossom and through a park filled with couples taking picnics and pulled up outside a cream townhouse in the east of the city. Its lower windows were almost obscured by a wisteria in high bloom that snaked up the building, blue flowers cascading down on to the balconies that sprouted from every floor. At one window, Maximilian noticed, the stems hung ragged as though they had been torn away from the wall.

"Madame Elise is my dearest, oldest friend," Madame Emerald told them as she pressed a finger to the doorbell. She glanced down at Maximilian and Oscar and smiled. "And I feel sure that one of these two splendid fellows will lose their heart to the beautiful Summer Rose."

A rather flustered footman met them at the door. After he had taken all their coats and dropped at least three of their hats he showed them into a dainty parlour in which a tiny woman was sprawled across a sofa, sobbing into a cushion. The footman blushed and coughed a little too loudly and the lady lifted her head.

"*Chérie!*" she cried and, leaping up from the sofa, she threw herself into Madame's arms. "Thank goodness you have come! My poor darling Summer Rose!"

Madame Emerald led Madame Elise to a seat and whisked a lace handkerchief out of her sleeve. The footman threw her a look of extreme embarrassment and shuffled out of the room. Sylvia and Agnes perched on a cornflower-blue sofa crammed with far too many cushions for comfort and shot one another looks that said "this is a little awkward".

"Is Summer Rose ill?" Madame Emerald asked, patting Madame Elise on the shoulder. The woman lifted her head and wailed one word, a word that made Maximilian's tail buzz.

"*Kidnapped!*"

"Kidnapped?" cried Sylvia and Agnes together.

Madame Elise waved a hand at a pile of papers strewn across a low coffee table in the middle of the room. "There have been an appalling number of cases this month. All beautiful animals, though none of them as beautiful as my little Summer Rose. And I'd just had a new portrait made of her too!"

Maximilian stared at the papers. On each there was a photograph much like the one he had seen of Winter Star: a beautiful cat sitting on a cushion or perched on a chair. His tail prickled. Somehow he was sure that there was something that linked them, but he could not work out what. They all looked so similar. What was it he was missing?

He glanced around the room. Every surface was covered in photo frames. There were carved wooden ones and plain glass ones, gleaming silver ones and antique ones on which the lustre was dulling. Every frame had a photo of the same cat in it, a sleek Siamese with sparkling, intelligent eyes. She peered out

of a hatbox as a kitten in one, and sat upright on a cushion in another. In each picture a diamond-encrusted collar round her throat stood out, a shimmering heart-shaped jewel hanging from it.

"Is this the new picture?" Madame Emerald asked, picking up an unframed photograph that had fallen to the floor. It was covered in tear stains and was a little crumpled around the edges. Madame Elise sniffed loudly and nodded her head.

"I had it taken only two days ago," she sobbed. "She was so good, sitting for her portrait, and I was going to have it framed in rose gold at Lucée's. I went to wake her this morning, and the window to her room was wide open and she had *gone*!"

Maximilian padded over to sit by Madame Emerald and inclined his head to get a closer look at the photograph she was holding. Summer Rose sat on a cushion, her head turned elegantly to the camera lens. He craned his head a little and his tail tingled at the sight of a new clue. Half-covered by Madame's thumb was a signature on the corner of the photograph that looked very familiar.

"She didn't make a single sound," Madame Elise was saying. "And none of the windows were broken. That's how I *know* it was one of the staff. She would have cried out if a stranger came into the house.

I've dismissed all the staff. All except Victoire, who let you in. He was away in the country till this morning, so I know it wasn't him. He's having to be cook, butler and housemaid, but he's coping admirably, and he did so love my little Summer Rose."

She dissolved into floods of tears again and Maximilian raised an eyebrow at Oscar. Now they knew why the footman was looking so frazzled. Maximilian slipped to the floor. "I think we should do a little detecting, don't you?" he asked as he passed Oscar, and the two of them padded out of the room and into the hallway.

Madame Elise had said that Summer Rose had disappeared from her room, but where on earth could her room *be*? And how could the thief have got in? "How might you get into a house without breaking a window?" Maximilian wondered aloud.

Oscar thought for a second.

"The wisteria that was so ragged on the front of the house as we drove up..." he began, but Maximilian was ahead of him.

"The left-hand side of the house, at the front, first floor," he hissed, and they sped up the stairs, took the left-hand bend at the landing and bounded into a small room at the end of the corridor.

Maximilian, before he had been fortunate enough to find his home at the Theatre Royal, had been brought up in what he thought was the height of luxury, but Summer Rose's room took his breath away. The carpet was so soft and plush that he sank into it to the top of his paws. The walls were decorated with paper, hand-painted with rose trellises. In the middle of the room sat an enormous velvet pillow, surrounded by soft silk curtains pulled back with satin rosebuds. A small bedside table held potions and powders that Agnes and Sylvia would have been envious of, and in the centre was a large jewel box with room for just one precious cat collar. It was open and empty.

"Of course, she may simply have run away," Oscar suggested.

"What cat would run away from this luxury?" Maximilian said, but even as he said it his conscience pricked him. He would not swap his life and all his friends in the Theatre Royal for a hundred luxurious cat beds, and the old velvet cushion that Mrs Garland had found for him to sleep on was the most comfortable one he had ever had.

Maximilian sniffed the air. In spite of all the roses there was an unpleasant smell pricking at his nose. He sniffed again. He was sure that the smell was coming from the window. Crossing the room (which was most difficult as his paws kept sinking into the carpet), he leapt up on to the sill. He had been right. The smell was stronger here. He sniffed again and his tail tingled at the same time that his head reeled. The busy Paris street swam a little below him.

Maximilian peered closely around the tiny balcony. To his left hung the wisteria branch with its roots ripped away from the wall. *What on earth could have caused that?* He wondered. He padded round the sill, but there was nothing except a candle in a silver jar, tipped over on its side, and a folded piece of glossy paper, torn at one corner. He pushed this around with one paw, but it did not seem to him to be much of a clue, so he batted it aside.

He nosed into a corner where the smell seemed stronger and something sour filled his nostrils, fighting against something tasty and sweet. Maximilian covered his nose with one paw and, reaching into the corner with the other, he dragged out a piece of meat.

Oscar sniffed the air. "What a curious smell!" he said. "What on earth is it?"

Maximilian swept the meat into the room. He leapt up on to the bedside table and whisked a handkerchief from a pile elegantly tied in a ribbon next to the jewel case.

"I've smelled this before," Maximilian said. "It smells like the drops those villains used to kidnap Madame Emerald last year. I think it has been drugged." He rolled the meat into a neat parcel. "We should show this to the humans. Together with the broken wisteria outside the window, I think it points to only one conclusion. Summer Rose was *not* taken by a member of Madame Elise's staff. The reason she did not cry out was because she was *drugged*, and whoever took her climbed up that wisteria branch to get into her room."

CHAPTER 7
The Whiskers Begin to Tingle

The humans, as usual, proved particularly slow on the uptake. Maximilian dropped the morsel of drugged meat in front of Sylvia and pawed at her ankle, but she only shooed him away with her foot and went back to patting Madame Elise on the arm. Agnes, who was rather ineffectually stroking the photo of Summer Rose and murmuring "poor puss-cat" over and over again, was also uninterested in the smelly portion. It was only when

Oscar pressed a paw against the meat so that the sourness leaked out into the room that the humans finally sniffed the air.

"What on earth is that smell?" Madame Elise cried.

Sylvia wrinkled her nose in disgust and glanced down at Max. He nudged the parcel of steak towards her and miaowed his "I think this is worthy of investigation" miaow. Sylvia whisked her feet away and squealed.

"Urgh, Max, what have you got there?"

Madame Emerald was far more sensible. Max knew he could rely on her. She had been very brave when he had first met her in London, shimmying down drainpipes and standing up to dastardly villains.

She leaned forward and peered at the morsel on the floor.

"My dear, if I am not mistaken, this is a piece of beefsteak." She sniffed the air and a shadow fell across her lovely features. "And I think it has been drugged."

After that it took them very little time to piece things together. Maximilian pulled at the hem of Sylvia's dress and they followed him upstairs, where he and Oscar drew their attention to the broken wisteria.

"And to think I thought it was one of my maids. When we have found my Summer Rose I will make it up to them. They will have a week's holiday and tea at Alfonse's and meringues from—"

Madame Emerald gently cut her short to suggest that she phone the *gendarmes* with the new information that Maximilian had found.

"You're a marvel, Max," Madame said as they drove away from the house. "You and your friend stopped Madame Elise from making a very unfair mistake."

"It's most peculiar that the latch on the

window wasn't broken by whoever stole Summer Rose," Sylvia mused. "I wish Max could solve that mystery."

"Someone probably forgot to close it properly," Agnes offered, and they agreed that this seemed sensible.

But Maximilian was not so sure. The kidnapper had known that Summer Rose would be in that room at the front of the house. They had known which window to climb in at, and that must mean that they had been in the house at least once before the kidnapping. Could they have been there just before the crime and left the window unlocked on purpose?

Maximilian and Oscar discussed the possibilities on the way back to the concert hall. It was a fine spring day and Paris was beautiful, but Maximilian was so engrossed in this new mystery that he hardly took in any of it. While Agnes gasped in delight over the pink blossom in bloom on the tree-lined avenues, Maximilian was pondering who could have had access to Madame Elise's house. While Madame pointed out the beautiful church of Sainte-Chapelle and described the stained-glass windows which were the finest in Paris, Maximilian was thinking about the wisteria's strong trunk and sprawling stems. And when Sylvia begged them to stop the car so that she could browse through boxes of silk-covered notebooks and photograph albums at a tiny stationer nestled in one of the backstreets, Maximilian and Oscar huddled together on the back seat and put their heads together.

"Madame Elise's wisteria is strong," Maximilian said, "but even so, could it bear the weight of a full-grown man?"

Oscar frowned. "There were quite a few stems that had pulled away from the wall," he said. "The trunk is strong, but to reach the balcony a thief would need to clamber across one of the smaller branches."

"So, it would be someone small," Maximilian mused. He sighed. There did not seem to be much to go on. Something in his whiskers tingled, the familiar sign that he was close to connecting one clue to another. He was sure that the photographs of the cats held a clue to the mystery, but still he could not work out what it was that they all had in common.

CHAPTER 8
Zelie

Maximilian and Oscar had not forgotten their promise to Peppi, and the next day they wandered through the city streets to find the grey cat's apartment. *Paris is very different to London,* Maximilian thought. Everyone's legs seemed to walk at half the speed, taking long strides instead of the neat hurried steps of London's crowds. There were cafés on every corner, at which ladies in simple but beautifully cut dresses sat drinking from tiny coffee cups and nibbling at pastries dripping with chocolate. They passed by milliners' shops, the windows full of extravagant hats overflowing with pleated silk and velvet flowers, or simply topped with a single peacock feather and jet beading. They lingered outside patisseries, where pyramids of cakes in every colour of the rainbow made Maximilian's mouth water, and shops where jewel-like sweets tumbled out of twists of paper. And everywhere they went, the filigree shape of Eiffel's tower followed them. Sometimes it peeped above the rooftops, only the top platform visible through the chimneys and trees. Sometimes it surprised them, appearing between the streets that led down to the river Seine.

"The tower really is splendid," said Oscar as they walked towards it through a beautifully kept park.

Maximilian agreed. It *was* beautiful, from its four great columns, sprawled like lion paws digging into the ground, up to the tower itself, swooping skywards, its iron girders criss-crossing over one another as it wove its way to the clouds. Maximilian could see dozens of visitors scurrying around inside like tiny mice. Thinking about mice made him think about food and how long it had been since breakfast, and whether there might be anything tasty at Peppi's house.

They found the pink house on the other side of the park. Far from being the "tiny apartment" Peppi had described, it was a beautiful townhouse six stories high. The front overflowed with flowers cascading down from window boxes groaning under their weight. A small cream van had drawn up at the door and, from the back, an elderly delivery man was unloading yet more flowers. Vase upon vase of pink roses came spilling out of the van and were passed to a frazzled-looking young boy who bounded up the steps to the front door to hand them to a stern maid.

"Put them over there, behind the cushions," called a voice from inside the house. Maximilian followed the sound and leapt up to an open window to peer in, followed by Oscar.

They looked into a small sitting room. Peppi sat on a pink velvet cushion that set off his beautiful grey fur to perfection. He was being carefully groomed by a girl in a striped apron while Madame Belfourte conducted an orchestra of flustered maids bearing swathes of ivy and vases bursting with roses. Beside her was a young woman dressed all in black. Her hair was slicked back against her head, one perfect round curl pinned above her right eye. She wore a monocle and stood with her arms crossed, the forefinger of one hand impatiently tapping against her arm.

The girl in the striped apron unfurled Peppi's

hair from six little rollers and brushed it so that it curled across the cushions. She teased a halo of fur into shape around his face and then, sheltering his eyes with her palm, picked up a cut-glass perfume bottle and spritzed his fur so that it shone beautifully in the light. Madame Belfourte clapped her hands and declared him to be perfect. The woman in black sighed and, picking up a camera from a nearby table, began to take picture after picture.

"This must be the famous Zelie," Maximilian said, watching the woman tweak the roses near Peppi's face and smooth a lock of his hair into a wave across the front of the cushion. She worked quickly, moving round the room to photograph him from above, looking up into the camera, then from low down, tilting a lamp to catch his face half in shadow. Finally, she stepped back and declared that she was finished.

"Unless..." she said, glancing round the room. She picked up a mirror and turned to Madame Belfourte.

"I wonder if we should try a picture of Peppi by the window," she said. "The light can be so lovely at this time of day." She clicked her fingers at the maid, who moved to pick up the cushion that Peppi was resting on and turned to the window.

"You seem to have a visitor, Madame," Zelie said, spying Maximilian.

"Oh, it is the little cat from yesterday!" cried Madame Belfourte, moving to the window. "The one who is such a good friend of our Madame Emerald."

Maximilian glanced to his right and realised that Oscar had slipped away. He never did much like to be around humans.

"What is it doing here?" asked Zelie.

"Perhaps he came to see Peppi have his photograph taken," said Madame Belfourte.

"Perhaps he hoped you would take his photo too."

She laughed, but Zelie tilted her head to one side. "Well, he *is* rather handsome," she said. "Not as handsome as Peppi, naturally," she added quickly, sensing Madame Belfourte bristle.

"I will pay for a portrait of him as a gift to Madame," said Madame Belfourte. "She would love a picture of her little friend, I'm sure."

Zelie nodded. She reached out of the window and in an instant Maximilian felt himself being lifted inside and deposited on a bright-blue stool by a piano.

"There," said Zelie. "Quite a contrast."

While the maid was arranging Peppi on his cushion by the window, Zelie fussed around Maximilian, teasing his hair out so that it looked extra fluffy. Maximilian began to wish that he had spent a little more time on his third groom this morning and that he had paid a little more attention to how grubby his paws were getting in the city streets He shook his tail out to make sure that it looked its best and lifted his chin to show Zelie what a noble, elegant cat should look like.

"Wonderful," she breathed and clicked away with her camera. Maximilian beamed. He glanced over at Peppi, but the little cat was not smiling back at him. Peppi looked most put out at no longer being the centre of attention. The maid who was combing his hair pulled a little too tightly and Peppi batted her rather petulantly with his paw.

"Oh, my poor darling," cried Madame Belfourte. "He is becoming tired, the precious baby." She looked at the clock on the mantelpiece and tutted. "I think maybe we have taken too much of your time, Mademoiselle," she said and, signalling to the maid that it was time for Maximilian to be put out, she swept Peppi into her arms. Maximilian found himself deposited outside, and the window was firmly closed behind him.

He peered through at Peppi and Madame Belfourte. Madame Belfourte was all smiles, directing her maids to help Zelie with her bags. Peppi was smugly happy that he was, once again, in the spotlight. But Zelie did not seem at all pleased. Her eyes strayed to the window once or twice while she and Madame Belfourte were talking, and Maximilian could tell that she was annoyed. Well, that was to be expected. The opportunity to photograph as handsome a cat as Maximilian would not come along every day. He whisked his tail in the air and leapt from the sill, feeling very pleased with himself.

CHAPTER 9
Salmon and Singing

Maximilian was still preening the next afternoon while Sylvia and Agnes bustled around, helping Minette get ready for the concert. Oscar had muttered something about Maximilian's head "taking up too much room" and had left for the roof to take in the Paris sights.

Agnes was pinning Minette's hair into a smart chignon and Sylvia was perched on the dressing table, painting the girl's nails with a pastel-pink varnish. On the dressing table was a coil of the shimmering lace that Mrs Garland had bought. She had cut a length as a present to Minette and promised to come back and pin it round the neckline of her dress before the concert.

"You really don't have to do this," Minette said, smiling at her reflection in the mirror.

"Mnf, we do," said Agnes through a mouthful of hairpins.

"Well, if you can get me looking one tiny bit as beautiful as Maximilian, it will be worth it," the girl said. "Just look at that tail of his! I don't know how he keeps it so splendid."

Maximilian beamed and drew his tail round himself with pride. After the photographic session he had felt much less like a clumsy Maximilian and more like an elegant, sophisticated Maximilian. His tail had been treated to no fewer than four grooms before lunch and six afterwards and he was sure that it looked its very best, fluffy and shining.

"Don't encourage him. He's already far too full of himself," Sylvia muttered, rather spoiling the moment.

There was a knock on the door of the dressing room and Agnes leapt to open it. One of the stagehands stood in the doorway, holding a large flat envelope.

"Madame Emerald said to give this to one of you young ladies," the boy said, looking admiringly at Minette. Agnes took the envelope and turned it over.

"Oh, Sylvia, look. It's addressed to '*the handsome cat of Madame Emerald*'!" she cried. She slid a hand into the envelope, drew out a flat piece of paper and gasped.

"It's a portrait of you, Max. Whenever did you have this taken?"

Sylvia held up the picture so that everyone else could see it. Maximilian sat perched on a bright-blue cushion. His fluffy white tail draped beautifully across the soft folds of the fabric and his eyes gazed wide and gleaming out of the photograph. In the corner was a signature written in a bold, brisk hand.

Sylvia read the back of the photograph.

"Cher Madame, I hope you will accept this photograph of your favourite young gentleman."

"It's beautiful, Max," Sylvia said. "I think we should give it back to Madame, though, don't you? After all, we'll have the original back with us in London."

Minette stood up, gave the daintiest of blows on her nails and held her hands out to admire them.

"They look wonderful!" she declared. "And your lovely Mrs Garland has promised to help me make my dress look a little different." She smiled at Sylvia and Agnes. "You've been so kind. I didn't think I stood a chance in this competition. I only entered this year because Madame Belfourte removed the entrance fee.

It was astronomic and only the best families could afford it. I don't think that Monsieur Pierre is happy about it at all. Well, thanks to you, I haven't looked too shabby. As soon as the concert is done, I am going to take you to see the city at its best, at night. We can go and see all the sights, and I'll take you to my favourite café."

Agnes gasped. "Paris by night! How romantic!" she cried.

Minette was as good as her word and, after the evening's concert was done, she swept them off to explore. She pointed out all her favourite spots and told them stories about the many landmarks they passed that rivalled even Oscar's tales. They wandered along the banks of the Seine, where Maximilian and Oscar felt a little resentful that there were so many rats to chase but no time to do so if they wanted to keep up with the humans. They admired the

Eiffel Tower, lit up with thousands of lanterns, and stopped on the bridges to watch boats full of revellers pass beneath. Finally, they arrived at Theo's, a neat café bar, overstuffed with tiny round tables at which too many customers were crammed. It was noisy and animated, with waiters dressed in black suits and cream bow ties darting between the tables.

Minette pushed open the door and a great roar came up from a table for four, around which at least nine people were crammed. The table groaned with carafes of wine and tiny plates of exquisite puddings drizzled in caramel and cream. A lady in a green tuxedo jumped up from the chair she was sharing with a woman in a black silk dress and threw her arms around Minette.

"*Ma chérie!* How was the concert? Were you divine as always?" she cried. Then, spotting Agnes and Sylvia over Minette's shoulder, she demanded to know who her new friends were. Minette introduced them all and there was a whirl as the table was rearranged and space was found for them all. Maximilian and Oscar were offered a chair between them and several customers squeezed up to allow Sylvia and Agnes to sit down.

Maximilian sniffed the air and sighed. It was thick with delicious aromas. The scent of salmon danced across the tip of his nose. Spiced almonds and honeyed apples tickled his whiskers. From across the room he caught a hint of oysters and the spark of wild garlic. He glanced at Oscar, who was carefully studying the menu propped up against a candlestick in the middle of the table.

"Max adores salmon," Agnes was saying to the waiter who had appeared at her elbow. She looked at Oscar and frowned. "We don't know about his friend, though..."

"Salmon would be delightful," miaowed Oscar politely and Agnes took his miaow to mean "yes".

"The salmon is sautéed in prawn butter," Oscar whispered to Maximilian, pointing at the menu. "Quite delightful."

Maximilian was watching Minette as she danced between the tables, talking with the customers at each. It was clear that she was very popular. A woman in a lace shawl pressed a small gift into her hand. A man with sideburns and the longest beard Maximilian had ever seen kissed her on both cheeks in a way that looked most tickly and threw his hands in the air, shouting, "The toast of Paris!"

At their table all anyone could talk about was how Minette was going to astound all of France with her voice. The woman in the green tuxedo was insisting to her neighbour that no one but Minette had a chance of winning the competition. The man next to her, swathed in scarves in spite of the heat of the room, declared there had not been such a voice since the great opera singer Célestine.

The salmon had just been delivered and squeezed on to the table in between seven half-eaten crème brûlées when a shout rang out from the other side of the room. "A song, Minette! A song for Theo's!" The whole room cheered in agreement and there was more hurried moving of the furniture while space was made for an old man at a rather rickety

piano. Minette was swept up on to a chair and, beaming around the room, she gave a little cough to clear her throat.

"Thank you all, my dear friends," she said. She motioned towards the man with the long beard. "I will sing this song for Monsieur Benedict. It reminds him of his wife when they were young together. It is an honour to sing it."

She nodded to the piano player and they began. It was a song of exquisite sweetness, perfectly suited to Minette's voice.

The audience hung on every note and when, at the last, Minette sang out a pure high note that tinkled against the wine carafes and danced round the glasses, there was a moment of silence and then the whole café rose to its feet in applause.

Maximilian looked round. Everyone seemed to be blinking back tears or dabbing their eyes. He glanced at Agnes, who was openly bawling, and Sylvia, who whisked a finger across her eyelashes and called out, "exquisite". Even Oscar appeared to have lifted a paw to his one good eye. Maximilian stared at Minette and was again sure of one thing. She *had* to win the competition. She *was* "The Voice of Paris".

CHAPTER 10
The Catnapper Strikes!

Everyone slept a little late the next day and it was not until nearly noon that they arrived at the concert hall to discover Madame Belfourte in an agony of worry, having read in the papers the report of the kidnapping of Summer Rose. She had taken to carrying Peppi everywhere she went and insisting, however much Pierre resisted, that the little cat could not be left backstage.

"We can clear a space for him on the desks at the front of the stage,"

Madame Emerald assured Pierre. "Or even ... under?" she suggested, but the look of thunder on Madame Belfourte's face made it clear that Peppi would not be reduced to sitting on the floor. Monsieur Lavroche offered to have Peppi in the box that he shared with Mrs Garland, but however much he assured her that they would look after Peppi just as well as they looked after Maximilian, Madame Belfourte would not be moved. Peppi was to stay with her.

Shaking his head in bemusement at all the fuss, Oscar crept off for a walk on the roof and Maximilian settled down under Madame Emerald's judging desk, ready to be delighted by the evening's concert and determined to think about what he and Oscar could do to investigate. It was a very difficult case. He had no suspects, no real clues, and no idea of what to try next. Maximilian sighed. Maybe he really *would* have to leave it to the *gendarmes*. How disappointing that would be.

Minette was first on stage. For a moment Maximilian thought that she had acquired a new dress, but then he realised that she was wearing the same one as before, cleverly tweaked so that the skirt fell in a cascade from one hip, and with Sylvia's beaded cream chiffon cape draped over her shoulders. Mrs Garland must have worked her magic once again to help Minette. Maximilian felt glad to have such kind and thoughtful humans as his dearest friends.

After Minette had finished singing a beautiful aria about a fairy-cursed milkmaid, Albert took to the stage. Beaming round the audience, he espied a particularly cheerful-looking lady in one of the boxes and directed his song towards her. The whole audience was charmed by Albert and as he finished his song and whisked a kiss to the lady in the box, the audience rose to its feet, the sound of applause thundering round the auditorium. Albert swept a glance around the room, smiling his thanks to everyone from the society gentlemen in the front stalls to the families crowded into the standing room galleries in the upper reaches of the hall. Ordinarily, Maximilian would have joined in, waving his tail enthusiastically in recognition of Albert's wonderful performance, but just as he was rising to his paws something caught his eye. To either side of 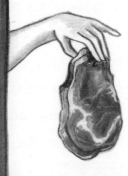 the stage were doors hung with thick curtains through which ushers with trays of chocolate and ices would come during the intervals. A small, slender hand had slipped through the slit of the curtains, a plump *filet* of beef dangling from its fingers.

Maximilian's mouth began to water. He took a step towards the morsel, but before he had moved even one cat-length the sour smell of it hit his nose and he felt his fur stand on end. Before he could miaow his "stay away from the beef, it could be drugged" miaow, he saw Peppi slip from Madame Belfourte's table and pad across towards the curtain. Madame Belfourte, deep in conversation with Madame Emerald, did not notice as her precious Peppi crept away from her. With a roar of "I will save you!" Maximilian dashed towards the curtained door and, overtaking Peppi, sprang at the mysterious hand and sank his teeth and claws into it. There was a shrill cry of pain and the hand was whipped away. Maximilian and the beef fell to the ground, where the first struggled to his feet and the second was set upon by

Peppi. Maximilian pushed his head through the curtain, hoping to see who had been trying to lure Peppi away, but all he saw was a figure dressed all in black flitting round a corner and out of sight. Maximilian was about to give chase when he felt himself being lifted in the air by satin evening gloves and turned to see the lovely face of Madame Emerald.

"What on earth are you up to now, Max?" Madame asked.

Maximilian began his "pardon me, but I need to apprehend a dastardly villain so would be very grateful if you could put me down" miaow (one of his most complicated) but was drowned out by a shrieking from Madame Belfourte.

"Peppi!" she cried. "My darling Peppi! What has happened to him?"

Peppi lay motionless at her feet.

CHAPTER 11
The Talk of Paris

After that there was a great deal of fuss. The thin-faced judge, Pierre, sprang up to the stage and announced that there would be a short interval before the next two performances. One of the stage crew descended on the comatose form of Peppi with a blanket and bore him away backstage, followed by a still distraught Madame Belfourte. A vet was called for and Madame stroked the grey cat's face, begging him to wake up. But Peppi's eyes remained closed and he did not stir even when Madame Belfourte softly sang the lullaby that she said was the little cat's favourite.

They had an anxious wait for the vet, a jolly-looking man who Maximilian suspected had been interrupted during his evening meal, if the fresh gravy stains on his waistcoat were anything to go by. There was another wait while he listened to Peppi's chest with a stethoscope and sniffed his breath. Finally, he patted Madame Belfourte on the arm and declared that in his opinion "this cat has been drugged."

Maximilian felt his tail tingle. He had been right! If only Madame Emerald had not stopped him from chasing after the perpetrator, he would have solved the crime by now. Instead he was sat in Madame's arms, being fussed over by Sylvia, who was worried that he might have eaten some of the beef himself. As if he would be so silly! Wriggling free, he leapt to the floor and dashed away to find Oscar.

🐾

"It was a very bold move," Oscar mused. "To actually make an attempt on a cat while their owner is in sight. Our thief is getting braver."

"Or more reckless," Maximilian said. "The other thefts all took place when the owners were safely out of the way."

"Pierre seemed most anxious to get Madame Belfourte away from Peppi," Maximilian said. "I thought that was very peculiar."

"But he was sat at the judges' table the whole time," objected Oscar. "He can't possibly be involved."

Maximilian frowned. Oscar was right, of course. However much he disliked Pierre he had to admit that the hand that had offered drugged meat to Peppi did not belong to him. Secretly he was a little disappointed. Anyone who disliked cats as much as Pierre did was *not* to be trusted and it would have been good to expose him as a dastardly villain.

"One thing is for certain," Oscar said. "Tomorrow morning the papers will be full of this."

Oscar was correct. The other catnappings had been small affairs, covered in the middle pages of the newspapers, but the events at the concert hall made all the front pages. The

attempted theft of a cat belonging to one of society's most influential patrons of music in the middle of Paris's most glamorous music hall and in front of thousands of people was tremendously exciting news. Soirées at the city's most fashionable houses were pushed to page two. A wedding between a count and the daughter of a sugar magnate slipped to page four. Instead, the papers were full of pictures of Peppi and the great revelation of the day – Madame Belfourte would no longer be the chief judge of "The Voice of Paris".

"And all because of that cat of hers!" Madame Emerald exclaimed, throwing down her copy of the newspaper in exasperation. They were sat at a table in Minette's café, but nobody seemed in the mood for breakfast. Sylvia had turned over the same *pain au chocolat* several times without taking a bite and even Agnes was showing no interest in the pile of croissants that had been placed in front of her. Madame Emerald sighed. "She is refusing to leave her house until the catnapper of Paris is caught." She glanced at Maximilian and her face softened. "We can't blame her really, I suppose. We would all be distraught if anything happened to Max. But really, it is infuriating! We have two days to go and we are now down to just two judges! Pierre says that he is looking for a replacement for Madame Belfourte but I hate to think who he will come up with. And if he can't find anyone, the competition will have to be cancelled."

There was a faint clatter of teacups as she said this, and Maximilian saw that Minette, who was serving a customer at a nearby table, had overheard them. If the competition was cancelled then she would lose her chance to shine and perhaps become a professional singer. Excusing himself, Monsieur Lavroche stood up from the table and went over to talk with her.

"I tried everything to persuade Madame Belfourte to stay," Madame Emerald sighed. "I wish someone could catch this wretched catnapper." She smiled sadly at Maximilian. "If only the *gendarmes* had Max on the case. He would solve it in two shakes of a cat's tail, I'm sure of it."

Maximilian gave his front paws a groom and tried to look modest, but it was lovely when Madame Emerald spoke admiringly of him with her beautiful, melodious voice. He wished he could assure her that the two cleverest cats in Europe were already following up several clues.

"Will the competition really have to be cancelled?" asked Mrs Garland. "It would be a shame after all the organisation, and half of the city seems to be after tickets."

Madame sighed.

"I suppose we *could* limp along with only two judges. But what if we disagree?"

"You could judge by the volume of the applause," suggested Sylvia. She winked at Agnes, and Maximilian knew that she had only suggested this because Minette and Albert were the favourites with the crowd.

"Well, I will talk to Pierre," Madame laughed. "But I am sure he will not be in favour of *that* solution. If only *we* could find another judge instead of leaving it up to him. Perhaps…"

"Monsieur Lavroche!" cried Agnes. "Oh, he would be *perfect!*"

"And *most* impartial," Sylvia assured her.

Madame sighed. "That might work. Oh, I will miss Madame Belfourte. Her judgement is always so good and Pierre is going to be *insufferable* as premier judge. He wants all the posters for tomorrow's concert reprinted with his name at the top, and he is demanding fresh flowers in his dressing room every day. He has been *desperate* to be premier judge. It's such an honour. I think he would have done anything for it to go to him. He was livid when it went to Madame Belfourte, although she really was the better choice. He is such a snob. Always on about how the competition should only be open to the best musical families, wanting to go back to charging an entrance fee only the richest competitors could afford."

Maximilian's tail twitched. He met Oscar's eye and raised an eyebrow. If Pierre was so determined to be premier judge, and so unhappy with Madame Belfourte's decisions in the role, then he had the perfect motive for scaring off Madame Belfourte so he could replace her. *Finally*, Maximilian thought, *we have a suspect.*

CHAPTER 12
An Unexpected Trip

The next morning Madame Emerald collected them for a special treat. It was the last day of the competition and there were to be two concerts, one of them in the largest park in Paris. On the way, as Madame chatted with Agnes and Sylvia, Maximilian shared his suspicions with Oscar. He had spent all night thinking things over, staring out of their hotel window at the city's beautiful lights, and he had ideas to share.

"Pierre *has* to be behind Peppi's

kidnapping," he declared. "Madame said that he was desperate to get rid of Madame Belfourte and I think he doesn't want Minette to win. If he is planning to replace Madame Belfourte with a judge as snooty as him then he *has* to do it before tonight."

Oscar frowned. "But you said that he was beside you at the judges table when it happened. So, it can't have been him behind the curtain."

"He must have an accomplice," Maximilian suggested. Something prickled at the back of his head. He was sure that there were clues that he was missing, if only he could make the connections. Whoever was kidnapping the cats was small and light enough to scale a wisteria and knew enough about the cats' houses to know how to get inside. His tail tingled as he remembered the photos of the missing cats. What was it about them that had caught his eye? He closed his eyes and pictured them in his mind. Each had a cat sitting on a comfortable cushion or sofa, a beautiful frame and in the corner...

"I know who the kidnapper is!" he gasped, making Oscar jump. "At least, I think I do. The pictures of the cats that were taken, in the papers, did you get a good look at them?"

Oscar nodded. "They looked like regular portraits of pampered cats to me," he said. "Why?"

"The signature in the corner," Maximilian said. "It was the same shape, a tall spiky start and a long, thin letter in the middle and..." He tailed off, but Oscar nodded enthusiastically.

"You're right, my friend, you're right. They were all taken by Zelie!"

"And if she has taken all the photographs of the catnapped cats..." said Maximilian.

"She would have been in the houses before they were taken, and would have had the perfect opportunity to quiz their owners on when the houses were likely to be empty!".

"And work out which windows would be the best ones to break into."

"And she is small enough to climb the wisteria!"

Maximilian felt his tail tingling. They were so close to solving the mystery. It must have been Zelie's hand behind the curtain at the theatre.

"So where does Pierre come into it?" asked Oscar.

Maximilian thought about this. Could Pierre be innocent after all, or were he and Zelie in league with one another? Maximilian did not like to dismiss Pierre so easily. He had a motive for kidnapping Peppi and he clearly hated cats, and that alone was sufficient to make him very suspicious indeed.

"There is only one way to find out," he said. "We must see if we can follow him at this afternoon's concert, and keep our eyes peeled for more clues."

The car turned into the park and came to a halt beside a stage by a lavish rose garden. Rows of white wooden chairs stretched out in a semi-circle, each topped with a satin bow and a small bunch of lily of the valley. The orchestra had arrived, but there were too many of them to fit in the space that had been provided for them. Concert preparations were plunged into chaos as seating was arranged and re-arranged. The trombonists argued with the cellists about who should get more legroom. The first violins

argued with the second violins about how close to the conductor they should be seated and the timpanist sneaked off to find an ice cream.

It had been Madame Belfourte's idea to hold one of the concerts outside, as a treat for those who could not get tickets for the main events and as a test of the singers' power, but with her gone there was so much to organise in so little time that no one noticed Maximilian and Oscar disappear behind a line of shrubs and set off across the park for a walk and to swap theories about the case.

It was a beautiful spring afternoon and the park was full of people enjoying the weather, strolling over ornamental bridges or lazing by the pools and rose gardens. Maximilian and Oscar headed away from the concert area, hoping to find a quiet spot, but half of Paris seemed to be out enjoying themselves. As they rounded the corner of a belt of trees that curved away from an aviary full of goldfinches, they found themselves in a wide open lawn. There were no fountains or pagodas and no ornamental lakes with swans and cygnets. Instead there were balloons – line upon line of brightly coloured balloons, each as tall as one of London's omnibuses, towering above them. Under each of them was a wicker basket hung with canvas bags and ropes and a team of men shouting to one another as they clambered in and out of the basket. The air roared with the sound of flames shooting up into the canvas of the balloons as they bobbed about, straining against the thick ropes that anchored them to the ground.

"Hot air balloons!" Oscar cried. "I wonder if they are going to race one another. Did I ever tell you about the time that I leapt from one hot air balloon to another mid-flight to retrieve the precious moonstone of the Countess of..."

But Maximilian was not listening to his

friend's story. His attention had been caught by something else. Standing underneath one of the trees on the far side of the park was a woman with dark, slicked-back hair and a monocle. She was pacing from side to side and looking at her wristwatch.

"It's Zelie!" said Maximilian.

"And that's Pierre!" Oscar said, nodding his head towards a thin-faced man who was dashing between shrubs to join Zelie by the tree.

Maximilian felt his whiskers buzz. Perhaps his suspicions that Zelie and Pierre were working together had been right after all.

"We need to get closer!" he cried and, without waiting for Oscar, he hurtled off across the grass to where Zelie and Pierre stood, deep in conversation. Zelie was glaring at Pierre, who was looking down on her, his face twisted into a nasty smile. How Maximilian wished he was close enough to overhear them. He had thought that the quickest route would be to cut straight across the lawns – what the humans liked to call "as the crow flies", though he preferred to call it "as the clever cat walks". But with every step they were tripping over the guy ropes anchoring the balloons to the ground, or stumbling on the great stakes driven into the ground to tie the ropes round, or snagging their fur as they squeezed past the wicker baskets.

They were just within earshot when Zelie flung her hands out to Pierre.

"I kept my half of the bargain," she said. "All I am asking for is a little co-operation."

Pierre laughed. It was not a nice laugh. "My dear, I'm not saying that I won't keep your little secret, and I'm very grateful to you."

"You're premier judge now!" she snapped. "Trying to kidnap that ridiculous cat of Madame Belfourte's worked. She'll never go near that concert hall again. You can save your precious competition and make sure the right person wins. So what else do you want?"

Pierre reached into his pocket and drew out a bundle of papers that he waved at Zelie. "I may think of something," he said and, folding the papers back into his pocket, he turned and walked away.

Maximilian's tail tingled. So he had been right! Zelie and Pierre were both involved, and it was clear that Pierre was planning to fix the competition so that Minette could not win. How dastardly! But knowing who was behind the crime was only solving half of the case. Where on earth were the cats? How could he save them? And what were the papers that Pierre had been waving at Zelie? With all these mysteries, Maximilian could feel that familiar tingling in the tip of his tail. Though, come to think of it, the tingling was a little different this time. It felt a little more like a pinching. Maximilian threw a look back at his tail and saw to his horror that it had become entangled in the weave of one of the baskets, and no matter how hard he tugged he could not free himself. He clawed at the basket to pull his fur away, but the ropes coiled round him, trapping him against the sharp wicker.

"Oscar! Help!" he cried.

In an instant his friend was at his side, but try as he might Oscar could not free Maximilian either. The basket began to sway from side to side and there was a jolt as it was lifted off the ground. Oscar flinched his head to one side as a rope whooshed past his ears and fell to the ground with a thud. The men in the basket cheered and there was a roar of flames. The basket swung violently to one side and began to rise into the air.

"My friend, hold on," Oscar said. "I think we are about to fly."

CHAPTER 13
A Flight Across Paris

From the ground, where Sylvia and Agnes were watching, the sight of a hundred hot air balloons taking flight all at once was breathtaking. The air was crammed with colour and flame as red and yellow balloons jostled with pink and green ones for space. Some of the teams threw ribbons from their baskets as they flew over the watching crowds, making them cheer with delight.

From the viewpoint of two terrified cats, however, the sight was breathtaking in an altogether different way. Maximilian and Oscar watched in horror as the ground sank away far beneath them, the basket they clung to swaying alarmingly and every jolt threatening to throw them to certain death. The other balloons swung dangerously close to them, the baloonists calling out to one another, spurring each other to go faster and higher. Maximilian sank his claws still deeper into the wicker basket and squeezed his eyes tight shut.

"It's a cat!" cried a voice from a basket nearby.

"No!" cried another. "*Two* cats!"

There were yet more shouts and Maximilian felt strong hands clasping him and his fur being disentangled from the sharp clutches of the wicker. Then he was being lifted gently into the air, a voice speaking calmly to him. He opened one eye and found himself face to face with a bearded man wearing a look of utter bemusement.

"A most handsome cat, but what on earth are you doing up here?"

"This one has been in the wars," said his companion, who had rescued Oscar and was holding him up for inspection. "Look at that eye. I bet he lost it duelling for a young lady cat's honour."

"Indeed I did," Oscar miaowed. Maximilian smiled wryly. Oscar had at least a dozen stories for how he had lost his eye, but this was his favourite.

"Well, cats, whoever you belong to, you will have to wait till the end of the race to return home. We must make up for lost time if we are to have a chance of winning," said a third man, who was working away at a series of pulleys underneath the balloon canopy. "And speaking of that..." He pulled on one rope and with a roar of flame the basket rose higher and shot forwards, past a basket full of women blowing kisses to the crowds below.

Maximilian miaowed his "but we were on the trail of a suspect and must get back to the ground at once" miaow, but the man holding him just laughed and lowered him on to a ledge that ran around the inside of the basket and served as a bench for its passengers to sit on.

Oscar leapt to join him, peered over the side and looked down. "No chance of getting out now, I'm afraid, my friend," he said. "We may as well just enjoy the view."

Maximilian had no intention of looking over the side of the basket. Much as he now loved his rooftop walks with Oscar, he was still not keen on heights that swung so alarmingly. He preferred the safety of a solid window sill or chimney pot. He remembered how he had laughed at Peppi for his nerves that first night they had taken him across the heights of Paris and felt thoroughly ashamed of himself. He was just as nervous now as Peppi had been then.

"Take a look down," Oscar said. "It really is the most incredible sight."

Maximilian opened one eye and gasped. From high up in the

balloon, Paris spread like a glorious map beneath them. In the park below, laid out in its neat squares and curved fountain walks, the people looked like small dolls. In a few minutes they had left the park and were soaring over the city, a carpet of cream stone and greenery. The balloon carried them over packed streets where shoppers jostled for fresh cheeses and meats, and above the curves of the beautiful Seine river, glittering in the spring sunshine.

As they were nearing the wonderful Eiffel Tower, whose top platform was crammed with tourists waving flags in a myriad of colours, eager to catch sight of the balloon race, Maximilian spotted a familiar figure far below, weaving nimbly through the crowds: a woman dressed in black with a yellow handbag. He was sure it was Zelie. She paused at the door of a house and, as she looked up to the balloons, the sun glinted off the monocle over her left eye.

"Oscar, quick!" Maximilian hissed. "That's

Zelie. We must remember how to get back here."

Oscar nodded and together they scanned the streets below. Oscar murmured to himself, "Two streets to the left of the river", while Maximilian memorised the sight of the stationer on the corner of the road and the wide, sweeping avenue that led down to a children's playground. He squeezed his eyes shut and found he could see a perfect picture of the streets below in his mind. He squeezed again, as if setting off a camera shutter, and then opened his eyes and looked at Oscar. They made a brilliant team. Zelie would be no match for them.

🐾

It was a few minutes later that the balloons finally began to descend towards an open piece of parkland in the west of the city. The sun was still high in the sky, and the white stone of the buildings surrounding the park glowed like jewels in the golden light. The balloons floated down in clusters, the cries of delight from the crowd and the race teams mixing with the sound of baskets bumping along the ground. The grass rose to meet them and as they thudded down three men rushed to steady the basket, slapping the team on the back and greeting them excitedly.

Maximilian grinned at Oscar and the two of them leapt from the basket, miaowing their thanks to the men who had rescued them. Then, being very careful to avoid being caught up in the ropes and baskets and canvases of balloons that were being deflated and falling with deep sighs to the ground, the two cats set off to find Zelie.

CHAPTER 14
Eloise

As they neared the house where they had seen Zelie, they heard her ordering one of the maids around as she had at Summer Rose's. The sound was coming from a room at the front of the house, by the door. Creeping closer and peering in they saw that she was arranging the room for a photo shoot. A plush cream velvet sofa was being set so that it perfectly caught the rays of the sun, which bathed it in a shimmering haze that made the soft silk fibres of the cushions bloom with warmth. Zelie stood fussing with her camera set up on a tripod, her back to the window.

"How perfect my Eloise will look there," gushed an elderly lady dressed in far too many layers of lace. "It's her favourite spot. We often put her basket there in the summer, she loves it so much."

"Really?" murmured Zelie, and Maximilian noticed her eye stray to a plush cat bed by the wide window.

The elderly lady waved a hand at a passing maid and after a moment's wait the most beautiful cat that Maximilian had ever seen was brought into the room. She had perfectly round blue eyes of such startlingly bright colour that they took Maximilian's breath away. Her coat was glossy and pale silver, with dark flecks of jet across her nose and the tip of her tail. The maid placed her carefully on the sofa and the sun's rays turned her silver coat to peach and made her eyes flash with a hidden fire under their cool blue. She was just settling her tail prettily under her front paws and purring politely to the maid who was brushing stray strands of fur out of her eyes, when her gaze met Maximilian's and her eyes widened.

Maximilian gulped.

"Wonderful!" Zelie exclaimed. She worked quickly, taking photo after photo while the spring sunshine flooded the room. Eloise was coaxed into tilting her head down to her paws or looking straight up into the camera, her eyes alert and flashing with light.

Maximilian thought that he had never seen a cat as lovely as her and he quite forgot that he was there on official detective business. He did not even think of the case until Oscar, bored with asking him what he could see and getting no response, swatted at his tail and demanded to know what *exactly* was going on.

"It's just as with Peppi," Maximilian said, ducking his head out of sight. "Zelie is taking plenty of photos, but she's not been left alone for even one second."

"I think I have as many photos as I need," said Zelie's voice from the front room. Maximilian raised his head over the window sill once more. Zelie was packing up her bags of equipment while a maid removed a cream satin ribbon from around Eloise's neck and replaced it with a necklace of shimmering sapphire beads from which hung a sparkling diamond "E".

"Well, I need to be getting ready soon," the lace-covered lady said. "I have been invited to the grand final of 'The Voice of Paris' competition tonight. Drinks at Maurice's and then a trip to the concert hall."

Zelie drew closer to the window.

"I left one of my lens cloths here somewhere," she muttered. Maximilian ducked away out of sight and saw her slide her hand under the window and slip something on to the sill.

"I'll close this for you if you would like, Madame," she called, pulling the window shut.

Maximilian caught Oscar's eye, and felt his tail tingle. The woman was definitely up to something. Something in her voice had sounded very calculating and he wanted a closer look at whatever she had left on the window sill. Being very careful not to be seen, he peered into the room. Zelie was leading the lace-festooned lady out into the hallway. Eloise sat on her cushion, grooming her front paws. Maximilian let out a small sigh and Oscar coughed gently and raised an eyebrow.

"She is certainly a most beautiful cat, my friend," he said sternly. "But I believe we are here on official business?"

Maximilian blushed and turned his attention to the window. The sill was painted sunshine yellow, some of the paint peeling a little at the edges, but a slice of white in one corner caught his eye. He reached out and nudged it with his paw.

"She's wedged something under the window," he miaowed to Oscar. "Look, it stops the catch from closing properly."

He peered closely at it and gasped. It was a folded piece of glossy paper. Maximilian's tail tingled again. Where had he seen something like this before? Of course! It was exactly like the piece that he had seen in Summer Rose's room and had dismissed as meaning nothing. How foolish he had been not to recognise it for the clue that it was.

Oscar nudged at the paper with his nose. "If I am not mistaken," he said, "that is photographic paper. Very easy for her to tear a piece up and wedge it under the window. That must be how she is planning on getting back in to take Eloise."

Maximilian felt a sudden chill. They had to warn Eloise that she was in danger! He tapped his paws on the window and miaowed frantically at her, waving his tail to get her attention. Eloise paused mid-paw wash. Her beautiful blue eyes widened still further. Then, smoothing a tuft of fur behind one ear, she leapt elegantly to the floor and padded across to the chair by the window.

Maximilian leaned down so that he could talk through the slim gap in the window frame. It necessitated sticking his bottom in the air and was not the most dignified way to meet a lady, but for once there were bigger things at stake than his dignity.

"You are in great danger," he said.

Eloise gave a little cry of alarm and took a step backwards. Maximilian felt rather silly for having started so bluntly, but he was not in the habit of warning young ladies of their impending kidnapping and was unsure of the etiquette.

"What my friend means," said Oscar, "is that we have fears that the lady you have just been entertaining intends to kidnap you, either this evening or in the very near future."

"Probably tonight, while your mistress is at 'The Voice of Paris' finale," said Maximilian.

They quickly filled Eloise in on everything they suspected. At first she was unsure, then amused, convinced that they were playing a trick on her. But once they pointed out the wedge of folded paper that Zelie had hidden in the window, she realised that they were telling the truth.

"Don't worry," Maximilian said. "We are going to save the other cats." He felt so heroic as he said this that he squared his shoulders and puffed out his chest, but the effect, with his bottom still stuck up in the air, was so comical that Eloise merely laughed, covering her giggles with her paw.

Maximilian sighed. It was very difficult trying to whisper through a tiny gap in a window and retain one's dignity. "We'll hide in the garden and wait till Zelie arrives," he said "then we'll follow her. You stay safely out of sight. Hide in your mistress' room, and don't eat anything she leaves in the house."

Eloise frowned. "But she might not go straight to the other cats without me," she said. "She will only take you to where the cats are if she has another to leave there."

Maximilian paused. She was right. There was only one answer.

"We'll think of something else," he said at precisely the same time that Eloise said the last thing he expected to hear.

"I'll go with her."

CHAPTER 15
A Stolen Song

Maximilian stared at her. It would be foolhardiness itself for Eloise to let herself be catnapped. Zelie was a very dangerous woman.

"You would be putting yourself in great peril," he said.

"And saving fellow cats," she said.

"But if we can move the paper so that the window closes properly then you will be safe," Maximilian objected. He placed his paw against the folded paper holding the window open and pushed hard, but it would not budge. He was about to try again when he realised that Eloise had her paw holding it fast on the other side.

"A cat does not run away from danger to save herself," she said.

Maximilian met her eye and realised that he was not going to win.

"Mademoiselle is right," Oscar said. "We will do all in our power to rescue you, Mademoiselle, but we cannot deny that there is a chance we will fail."

Eloise nodded. "Three clever cats against one human?" she smiled. "I think there is every chance that we will succeed."

"A remarkable cat," Oscar said on their way back to the theatre. Maximilian was silent. Secretly he was very worried. What if they lost sight of Zelie and Eloise was left captured and alone? He would feel responsible. As they reached the door of the Opéra Musique,

Oscar said, "I am sure Mademoiselle Eloise is correct, my friend. Working together we will foil this woman."

Maximilian nodded, but he could not shake the worrying feeling that he was leading them all into great danger. He wanted to seek out a quiet spot and plan out every detail in his mind, but the minute he entered the concert hall, Sylvia and Agnes swooped down on him and Oscar.

"We thought you'd been catnapped!" cried Sylvia, scooping him up into her arms and burying her face deep in his soft fur.

"We were about to call the *gendarmes*," scolded Agnes, dangling Oscar under her arm in a rather ungainly fashion. "We looked everywhere for you both."

"Neither of you will be let out of our sight till we are back on that boat to London," Sylvia announced.

Maximilian miaowed a frantic "but I have

144

a dastardly crime to solve" miaow, but Sylvia and Agnes ignored him, as usual, and he and Oscar were dragged away to sit in the dressing rooms with them while Minette prepared for the evening concert, the grand finale of the competition.

If Maximilian had thought that they would be able to sneak off, he was mistaken. Agnes and Sylvia were as good as their word and every attempt to leave the dressing room was scuppered by one of the girls. Agnes spotted Maximilian's attempt to slip around the legs of Madame Emerald as she did her nightly round of the dressing rooms to wish all the competitors luck. Sylvia caught Oscar trying to sneak away while they were all crowded round the mirror choosing a hairstyle for Minette. Eventually, Agnes shut the door of the room and, picking up both cats, placed them firmly on a cushion on the dressing table.

Maximilian watched the clock tick slowly round, his heart sinking. Zelie could be planning on taking Eloise at any time from the start of the concert. They had to get out of the theatre and back to her house.

At six o'clock there was a knock on the door.

"Come in," Minette called, but there was no response. After a few minutes Sylvia went to open it and found Pierre standing outside, his jacket slung over one shoulder. Maximilian rolled his eyes. It was so like Pierre to refuse to open a door himself. Ignoring Sylvia, the man swept past her into the room. He dropped his jacket on the back of a chair and sat down.

"I need your music for this evening, Mademoiselle," he said. "Need I remind you that any lateness will result in instant disqualification."

"Yes, Judge," said Minette.

"*Premier* judge," Pierre reminded her with a smile.

Maximilian grimaced. The man was insufferable. Still, this was an excellent opportunity to investigate what he had in his pockets. Perhaps the papers he had flourished at Zelie earlier would still be there? Taking

care not to be seen, Maximilian leapt to the floor and crept round behind Pierre. He edged a paw into Pierre's pocket and peered in. It was stuffed to bursting with pictures torn from newspapers, and they were all of the missing cats. On each of the photos the broad signature of Zelie was circled with a red pen. Maximilian felt his whiskers buzz as he pieced the clues together. Pierre must have worked out what he and Oscar had – that Zelie was behind all the disappearances. Was that what he meant when he told her he would "keep her secret"? Had he realised that and then asked her to kidnap Peppi?

Maximilian was shocked. The correct behaviour for anyone who stumbled across a dangerous kidnapper was to inform the police at once. Maximilian was just delving deeper into the pocket when Pierre stood up and whipped his jacket away and over his shoulder. Maximilian whisked his paw away and tried to look as though he had been innocently washing it.

"I'd better take my music down," Minette said as Pierre swept out of the room. She opened the top drawer of her dressing table, drew out a smart leatherette folder bound with twine and set off for the stage with Sylvia and Agnes in tow. For one glorious moment Maximilian thought that he and Oscar were going to be left alone, but Sylvia quickly squashed this hope by heaving him over her shoulder while Agnes swept Oscar into a cuddle that looked most uncomfortable indeed.

As they reached the end of the dressing-room corridor, Minette paused. From the auditorium came the sound of a beautiful love song, full of high trills and swooping cadenzas. The blood drained from Minette's face and she looked as though she was going to faint. With a little cry of "Oh no, no" she set off at a run for the stage. Sylvia and Agnes followed, Maximilian letting out a "mrowl" of annoyance as he found himself bumped along on Sylvia's shoulder. Minette ran out on to the stage where Julienne was mid-song, her arms lifted to the galleries. Minette let out a horrified gasp and Julienne turned. Maximilian saw a look of triumph pass over her face and she took a deep breath and carried on singing.

"What is it?" Sylvia asked. "What's wrong with that song?"

Minette bit her lip to try to stop herself from crying. "It's *my* song," she said, in a voice that was barely a whisper. "It's the song I was planning to sing as my final piece."

"But surely that's a song for a soprano," Agnes said. "Just listen to all those top C's." Maximilian heard the sigh in her voice as she said this and knew that Agnes had been thinking how wonderful it would be to sing it herself.

Minette shook her head. "It's written for a

low voice like mine. It's from my favourite opera. I didn't think that Julienne would choose it, but she must have had it rewritten to suit her own voice."

Maximilian's whiskers prickled and he glanced at Oscar. He had not imagined that cruel look on Julienne's face. She had known that Minette was planning to sing this song. She must have got hold of Minette's music folder and somehow stolen her song.

"I'm sure whatever you choose to sing instead will be lovely," Sylvia said, but Minette shook her head.

"It was my best piece and I really thought I had a chance of winning with it. I don't have anything half as lovely. Julienne will win for sure now."

"It's the singer, not the song," Agnes said firmly, but try as they might they could not cheer Minette up. They spread the music from her folder out across the side of the wings, ignoring

Julienne's laugh as she stepped over them on her way to her dressing room, and tried to find something else for Minette to choose for her final performance.

Maximilian saw his chance. Sylvia and Agnes were poring over the music sheets, Agnes humming along as she expertly read each song. Sylvia was looking at her with the same admiration that Agnes's face wore when she watched Sylvia dance. Maximilian felt a little disloyal for not staying and helping them choose. Clearly a cat with taste would be a useful asset at such a time, but with Eloise's safety at stake he was needed elsewhere. He winked at Oscar and, padding as softly as they could, they made their escape.

They fled across the city, dodging between the feet of people heading out for suppers in bistros or café bars and, risking their tails, dashing between the wheels of passing motorcars. As they neared Eloise's home, Maximilian saw that the sun was beginning to set, pink and peach rays spreading out across the sky. The lace-covered lady would be heading out for her elegant cocktails very soon, leaving Eloise all alone in the house.

"Hurry," he urged Oscar, and they picked up speed, racing down the wide avenue towards Eloise's house. They jumped over the low wall into her garden and dashed to the window. Maximilian leapt to the window sill and his heart sank. The white wedge of folded paper had gone from the window and it was locked shut. The sofa with the velvet cushions was empty and there was no sign of Eloise.

They were too late.

CHAPTER 16
A Chase Across Paris

Maximilian let out a howl of dismay. Eloise could be anywhere in this huge city and they had no way of finding her. He dashed to the road, desperately hoping that he might spy Zelie creeping round a corner, but there was no sign of her.

"We've lost her!" he cried. "How could we be so foolish?"

But Oscar did not respond. He was staring at something on the ground, something round and twinkling.

"Isn't that a bead from her collar?" he asked.

Maximilian leapt on the bead. It was a shining sapphire, milled into a perfect orb. The light of the setting sun danced in the heart of it. Oscar was right. It was exactly like the sapphires that were on Eloise's beautiful collar, the one with the diamond "E". Her collar must have come loose when Zelie was taking her from the house. Maximilian looked at the sapphire in his paw and felt his tail tingle. Surely if Eloise's collar had broken there would be more of the beads scattered around, not just one? Something in the back of his mind made him think that this had been left deliberately. He looked around, his eyes scanning the ground. At the edge of the garden gate something glinted.

"There's another!" he said, dashing over to the stone and rolling it in his paw. His tail tingled again and a spark of hope rose in his heart. He leapt over the wall and stared down the street. At first he could not see what he was looking for and he began to wonder whether he had been mistaken, but then there was a sparkle from under a hedge at the end of the street.

"It's a trail!" he cried, beckoning to Oscar to follow him. "Eloise is telling us to follow her!"

Together they dashed down the road, eyes hungrily searching out the sapphires. Some of them were easy to spot, glinting under

lamplights as the skies above darkened, but to his frustration Maximilian found that they often had to stop and look around before their eyes managed to seek out one of the inky-blue stones against the grey of the street.

It was as they turned a corner on to a wide avenue lined with trees that they saw a figure in black hurrying away, a large box swinging from her hand. Something small and glistening fell from the box, light flashing out as it bounced on to the pavement.

"It's her!" Maximilian miaowed, and the two cats pressed on, their paws flying along the road as they hurried to catch up with Zelie and Eloise. In a few moments they were gaining on her and could see clearly that the box she held was a cat basket. Eloise's face appeared at the grille in the side and she waved a paw and miaowed "not too close, she'll see you."

"Shush," snapped Zelie. "Awkward creature. Why didn't you eat the beefsteak? You greedy beasts usually gobble it up."

Maximilian and Oscar hung back a little and Zelie turned into a wide square under Paris's great cathedral of Notre-Dame. It towered above them, the lamplight picking out the stern faces of the figures that lined the arches and loomed over the doorways. Zelie crossed the square and slipped round the side of the cathedral, heading for a small arched door on one side. She drew a key from her pocket and, looking around to check that she was not being observed, slipped through the door.

Maximilian and Oscar dashed forward to catch it with their paws before it closed on them, but they were too late and the door swung back into the wall. Maximilian hissed in annoyance. The church had hundreds of windows, but none of them looked like the opening sort. He was about to say as much to Oscar when a glint of light in the doorway caught his eye. He peered closer. It was a perfect round sapphire bead. Eloise had dropped another, but why? Maximilian leaned closer and realised that the bead had fallen between the door and the frame, wedging it open just enough to stop the catch from clicking into place. Eloise had saved the day again.

He let out his "what a brave and resourceful cat" miaow and pulled at the door with his paw, but it would not budge. It was solid oak and far too heavy for a small cat. Even with

Oscar's help it was some few minutes before they managed, with huffs and groans, to pull the door open far enough to squeeze through. They found themselves in a narrow passageway with a winding staircase. Far above them they heard the soft echoes of footsteps as Zelie made her way up through the tower. Maximilian put a paw on the bottom step and began to climb.

🐾

The cathedral's tower seemed to go on forever and the staircase wound so tightly that after a few minutes Maximilian began to feel quite dizzy. After a while they came out on to a narrow balcony high above the city. Dark figures loomed above them and, looking up, Maximilian had to stifle a miaow of alarm. Above him, hunched over a narrow stone ledge, a skeletal creature with horns and sunken eyes hunkered down, watching the city below. Along from this nightmarish shape, the long beak of an enormous bird pierced the stone. Maximilian pressed himself against the wall of the cathedral, hoping that the creatures would not spot him.

"They are just gargoyles, my friend," hissed Oscar behind him. "The famous gargoyles of Notre-Dame de Paris. Stone figures, but very alarming for the unwary."

Maximilian did not have the time to feel foolish. With a quick nod of thanks to Oscar, he pressed on after Zelie along the balcony and through a passageway into the tower.

Above them, suspended between a network of rafters and ropes, hung a cluster of bells. Something mouse-like scuttled in the gloom, making Maximilian's whiskers tingle. Dust motes floated through the stale air and, from above, Maximilian heard the creak of wooden floors and the faint cries of a cat. No, not one cat, and not the soft lilt of Eloise's voice. This was several cats – some old and croaky, some young and mewling, and all of them crying the same things: "hungry", "thirsty" and "home".

CHAPTER 17
The Bell Tower of Notre-Dame

Maximilian and Oscar crept up the wooden stairs that ran round the inside of the bell tower. A cat's cradle of wooden beams criss-crossed over one another around them. The ropes of the bells hung between them, tiny mice running up and down, leaping from bell to bell.

Maximilian paused at the top of the stairs. Peering between the rafters, he could see Zelie's feet, clad in smart evening slippers. She leaned down and placed the cat basket in which Eloise was trapped on the dusty floor. From the basket next to hers came a plaintive mew and a tortoiseshell paw clawed its way out of the lid.

"Shut up, you little rats," Zelie snapped. "You're far too far up for anyone to hear so you may as well save your breath."

She clicked open the catch of Eloise's basket and dragged her out by the scruff of her neck. Maximilian let out a low growl.

"Where's that beautiful collar of yours, you wretch?" she muttered. She leaned down to shake the basket and a satin ribbon fluttered down to the floor, followed by a sparkling "E". Zelie snatched at them.

"The sapphires!" she snapped. "Where have they gone? They must have been worth a fortune."

She stuffed Eloise roughly back into her basket, ignoring her mew of pain as the wicker caught at one of her paws. Then she carefully threaded the diamond "E" back on to its ribbon and slipped it into her purse.

"You'll have to wait to be fed tonight," she said. "It's the last night of that silly singing competition and I promised that ridiculous Pierre that I would be there to photograph Julienne once he has made sure she wins. Oh, and I have these to deliver to your owners!" She brandished a pile of envelopes in the air. "A thousand francs each and I *might* think about giving you back to them. If they don't pay up, of course … well, if you're very well behaved I won't just leave you up here to starve."

Maximilian's blood went cold. The woman was a monster.

Zelie glanced at her watch, gasped, and turned on her heel towards the stairs.

Maximilian and Oscar had just enough time to leap down them, three steps at a time, and crush themselves into a dark corner before she appeared. Maximilian pulled his tummy in extra tight and sat on his tail to keep it out of sight. This was no time to worry about the dust it would be accumulating. Zelie sped past, muttering about lateness and changing, kicking up a flurry of dust that tickled the back of Maximilian's nose. He clamped a paw over his mouth and desperately tried to stifle the sneeze that he could feel building up.

Somewhere far below them, a door banged shut.

"Achoooo!" sneezed Maximilian, sending a nearby mouse scuttling up a rope. There was a flurry of excited miaows from the cats above.

"Who is that?"

"Can you help?"

"That dreadful woman has kidnapped us."

Then, above them all, Eloise's soft voice.

"Is that the English cats?" she asked. "Did our plan work?"

Maximilian bounded up the stairs.

In the octagonal
space above
the bells were
a dozen wicker
baskets. Cats
stared balefully
out of each,
some mewing
sadly, others
curled up, their
heads resting
listlessly on
their paws.

Maximilian
and Oscar got
to work. First
they freed Eloise.
With a quick
miaow of thanks,
she dashed
to the door

of a basket holding an elderly cream cat with nutmeg paws and unclasped the latch.

"Madame Margarethe," she cried. "I had no idea you had been kidnapped. Take my paw, Madame, if you need help to get down the stairs."

As the three cats worked to free the others, fresh stories of the horrors they had endured were shared.

"She didn't bring a proper basket!" a tortoiseshell cat cried, stretching his legs painfully after being released from the cramped basket he had been stuffed into. "I've been in that lunch basket for a week. I could hardly turn round in there."

"My poor kittens will be missing me so much," sobbed a fluffy cinnamon-coloured cat. "I haven't seen them in two weeks."

The cat called Margarethe patted her paw and murmured soothingly to her while Maximilian wrestled with the stiff clasp on an intricate basket in which a grey cat sat.

"You're Winter Star, aren't you?" he asked. "It was your owner who first put us on to this mystery." Maximilian was wise enough not to mention where he had heard of Winter Star's kidnapping. No cat would wish to hear that their owner had been out at the theatre while they were missing.

"I miss her so terribly," the cat said. "The food here has been simply awful, and all these other cats are far too noisy. Some of them never stop crying."

"Do you blame us?" asked a tiny ginger and cream cat, barely more than a kitten. "Poor Zizi has been shut up here for almost five weeks." He motioned to a jet-black cat who was helping Eloise to unclip a peach-painted basket in which a Siamese cat was impatiently clawing at the lid. It was Madame Elise's cat, Summer Rose.

"We'll get you all out of here," said Maximilian. "You can all go home now."

"Home?" asked Eloise." I'm not going home. I'm going to the concert hall."

Maximilian stared at her.

"If we work together, we can bring that woman to justice," Eloise said. "We owe it to Zizi and the other cats."

"She stole us from our homes," said Winter Star.

"And she took our collars," added the ginger and cream cat. "And goodness knows what she was planning do with us."

Maximilian looked around the bell tower. "There are fourteen of us," he began, a plan forming in his mind, but Eloise cut him off.

"Fourteen?" she said. "I think we can do better than that."

CHAPTER 18
The Cats of Paris

They fled the tower, the younger cats helping the older ones as they ran down the rickety stairs, across the balcony and down towards the wooden door that would let them out into the Paris night. At the door, Summer Rose jumped up to the catch on the handle and clicked it open. The rest of the cats hurled themselves at the door, forcing it open wide enough for each to slip through.

Oscar tripped down the stairs last, a red ribbon clasped in his teeth. An oval bronze medallion hung from it.

"A cat collar?" Maximilian asked, but Oscar shook his head.

"I think it was left by one of the bell-ringers," he said, dropping it to the dusty floor. "It has a picture of the cathedral etched on to it."

"But why?"

"We may need something that points to where all these excellent creatures have been, my friend," Oscar said. "What use is freeing them if we cannot bring their kidnappers to justice? I went looking for a clue and this was the best I could find."

Maximilian looked at him admiringly. Oscar thought of everything. The black cat slipped the medallion over his neck and together they crossed the courtyard, tiny shadows flitting through the moonlight, and set off across the city for the concert hall.

As they passed into the parts of the city where the houses were set back behind elegant curved railings, Eloise and the other cats began to dash up to windows and miaow through doors. Dark shapes slipped out into the night and joined them. Zizi scrambled up a tree to a balcony and miaowed with gusto till she was joined by four cats, who leapt from bough to bough and ran out on to the street.

As they moved by the river they were joined by rough-looking cats that Eloise and her friends did not know, but who were keen to help. They passed Peppi's house and Maximilian hurried to the window to call for him. As they leapt the low wall of his garden they heard crashes within his house and the front door flew open, revealing Madame Belfourte, holding a cup of tea and calling for Peppi to come back.

The cats ran on through the city – twenty, thirty, forty of them. They leapt over the tables of the street cafés where couples were chatting over coffee and wove between the feet of those out for an evening walk. The ever-growing tide of fur and fury flew over the bridge leading to the concert hall and flooded into the grand lobby, up the thick green carpet and through the doors to the hall itself.

Down on the stage, Henri was halfway through a solo. His face froze in shock and the notes died away in his throat as the doors were flung open and dozens of cats burst into the room, their miaows echoing and multiplying as they cascaded down the stairs. Ladies cried out in surprise as the cats jumped across the backs of their seats or ran between their feet. One of the cats leapt across the pianist's keyboard, setting off a cacophony of clashing notes that filled the concert space. Maximilian

led the charge to the stage, followed by Oscar and Eloise. Behind them, huffing and puffing, came Madame Belfourte, still brandishing her teacup and calling out for Peppi.

"What on earth is going on?" demanded Henri, aiming a sharp kick at Oscar, who jumped out of the way and glared at him.

Maximilian scanned the audience. Zelie must be here somewhere. He spotted her creeping out of the second row, gathering up her belongings and heading for an exit.

"There she is! Stop her!" he cried, hurling himself off the stage on to the judges' table. Madame Emerald gasped as he landed on her performance notes, scattering them. His paws skidded on the papers and he knocked a jug of water into the lap of Pierre but there was no time to apologise. Gaining his balance again he sped across the table and down on to the floor. Rounding the end of the first row of seats, he leapt towards Zelie, sinking his claws into her arm. With a cry she dropped her evening bag, which burst open. The diamond "E" of Eloise's collar twinkled in the lamplight.

"Get off, you mangy brute!" Zelie snarled.

She took hold of Maximilian by the scruff of the neck and threw him to the ground. She made a grab for her evening bag, but Eloise was too quick for her, springing on top of it and hissing. Three cats danced nimbly across the back of the chairs in the front row and wound themselves round Zelie's feet. The rest crowded round her, snarling, hissing and giving out low, threatening yowls.

"What on earth is going on here?" demanded Madame Emerald, striding across from the judges' table. Behind her, Pierre was looking from Madame Emerald to Zelie. A stern-looking woman in ruby velvet stood beside him. Pierre had clearly found his replacement judge.

Not for the first time, Maximilian wished that the humans could understand Cat. He tried his most understandable "Zelie is behind all the kidnappings and is extremely dangerous and duplicitous" miaow, but as usual Madame just stared at him uncomprehendingly.

"Where on earth did all these cats come from?" she cried.

"The river, probably," snapped Pierre. "Look at them. Probably riddled with fleas. Ugh, it makes me itch just to think of it." He looked round at the front rows of the concert hall and the ladies in their fine dresses drew their feet up from the floor.

"Nonsense," said a voice from the box above them. "That is my darling Eloise!"

It was the lace-draped lady from Eloise's house, staring down at them with surprise. Eloise miaowed a greeting to her.

"That is Winter Star," cried a man at the back of the stalls. "Where on earth has she been all these weeks?"

"That's my Zizi," shouted a woman in pink

satin, dashing down the aisle as fast as she could in her rather voluminous evening gown. "She has been gone for over a month!"

Zizi hurled herself into the woman's arms and she smothered the black cat with kisses, tears running down her face.

The concert hall exploded into noise as owners dashed down to find their cats. Winter Star's owner dragged two little girls covered in layers of organza behind him and they scooped Winter Star up and took turns to fuss over her. The tabby, Mathilde, leapt into the arms of a chic young woman in the third row. An elderly lady in a bath chair was wheeled down the aisle to claim the cinnamon-coloured cat.

"The stolen cats," Madame murmured. "But where did they come from?" She looked at Max and raised an eyebrow. "Max, did you rescue them? Oh, you *are* a wonder." There were mutters from the audience members closest and a smattering of applause, but Maximilian did not hear it. His mind was racing. How could he make Madame realise that it was Zelie who was behind the kidnappings? Never had he felt so helpless at not being able to communicate with the humans. He could not hope that they would notice the connection between Zelie's photographs and the missing cats. No one was looking at Zelie, except Pierre, who was still watching her nervously.

Maximilian's brain buzzed and then he felt his whiskers tingle. He looked across at Eloise. She nudged Zelie's bag towards him and one of the envelopes she had stuffed into it slipped out. In a moment he knew how he could make the humans realise.

With a great miaow of "look at this!" Maximilian pounced on Zelie's evening bag and dragged it across to Madame's feet. He pawed at her ankle and miaowed even louder. In the corner of his eye he saw Zelie tense. She edged closer to the exit. The cats hissed warningly.

"What is this?" Madame said, leaning down to pick up the bag. As she did so, one of the envelopes fell out and the letter in it fluttered to the floor. Madame picked it up.

"Winter Star is safe, but her safety depends on you," she read. "She will be returned to you if you follow these instructions…" Madame gasped. "This is a *ransom note*! Whose bag is this?"

She reached into the bag and drew out a handkerchief, a notebook and a smart business card. It was edged in black and on one side, embossed in gold letters, was the address of Zelie's studio.

Madame Emerald's face darkened and she glared at Zelie.

"You have some explaining to do, Mademoiselle," she said.

CHAPTER 19
Cat Cornered!

Zelie's bottom lip quavered. She looked desperately from Madame Emerald to the cats, to the crowd who were beginning to murmur and shake their heads. Someone in the upper gallery booed.

Now if I can only show that Pierre was involved too, thought Maximilian. There was nothing to connect the man to the cats, however. Or was there? Maximilian's tail tingled. He remembered the pictures of the cats torn from newspapers in Pierre's jacket pocket. Surely they would prove that he was more interested in the catnappings than he wanted to admit?

Maximilian bounded over to Pierre and jumped on to the chair beside him. He thrust his paw into the pocket of the man's jacket and, spearing the scraps of newspaper with his claws, dragged them out in one deft movement. They flew up into the air and fell like confetti around the feet of Madame Emerald.

"Get away, you little rat," Pierre snapped, swiping at Maximilian. Madame glanced at the pictures around her feet.

"But this is Summer Rose," she said, stooping to pick up the picture of the Siamese cat. "And here is Winter Star, and all the other cats who were stolen. Why on earth do you have these photos, Pierre?"

Zelie bounded forwards. "He was behind

it all!" she shrieked. "He talked me into it, but I never harmed a single hair on any of their heads."

"That's not true," Pierre shouted back. "*She* planned the whole thing. You've all made her very famous with those photographs of your ridiculous pets. Every newspaper in the land is carrying them now. She's made a fortune out of you and your pampered wretches. And she was going to make even more money once she collected the ransom money!"

"And you didn't tell *anyone* that you knew?" Madame Emerald demanded. "That is a despicable way to behave. Those poor cats have been missing for weeks!"

"Why would he tell anyone when he could get me to steal Madame Belfourte's ridiculous cat?" Zelie scoffed. "The moment he realised it was me taking the cats he couldn't wait to use me to get rid of that silly woman as premier judge."

There was a gasp from Madame Belfourte and a tiny tinkling crash as she dropped her teacup.

"Pierre! I thought you were my friend."

Pierre turned on her with a snarl.

"You always were particularly silly, Madame," he snapped. "There was no way I was going to let you continue to ruin this competition with your ridiculous ideas. Singing in the open. Letting *waitresses* enter! Can you imagine what a laughing stock the Opéra Musique would have been if that that girl won 'The Voice of Paris' over voices from some of the oldest music families in all of France?" He gave a shudder and glared at Minette, who, together with the other contestants, had poked her head round the edge of the stage curtain. Maximilian saw Julienne give a nasty smirk. Albert put an arm round Minette's shoulder and glared at Pierre. The judge in ruby velvet tutted, "Quite so."

Maximilian let out a hiss. Pierre was a horrible snob. *I bet he's behind the stealing of Minette's song*, he thought. *She would have been able to present her music before Julienne if he hadn't delayed her...*

Madame Emerald had heard enough. "Monsieur Lavroche," she said sternly. "I think it is time that we summoned the gendarmes." She turned to Maximilian and smiled. "It looks like you've saved the day again, Max. I wish we could know how you did it."

"Well, if you'd bother to learn Cat..." Maximilian miaowed, but Oscar nudged his paw.

"Your humans are very clever, my friend, but let's not expect miracles."

As Zelie and Pierre were hauled off by the *gendarmes* the cats returned to sit with their owners. The street cats crept into cosy corners by the side of the stage, enjoying the warmth of the hall and the comfortable plush carpet. Maximilian was pleased to see that the doormen did not shoo them away and that, one by one, they were welcomed on to the laps of concertgoers. "I'm sure we can find space for just a couple more at home," said one old gentleman to his stern-looking wife as Maximilian passed their seat, where a tortoiseshell and a ginger cat were curled up on the floor. In the front row, a tiny lady had gathered more cats than she had space for on to her lap. They were all very scruffy-looking, battered and wary from lives on the street. A sweet-looking tortoiseshell with a pretty round face and three legs was making herself at home tucked under the lady's arm.

Maximilian and Oscar bounded up the steps to the stage after Sylvia and Agnes, and Madame Belfourte returned to her seat at the judges' table. Henri took his place by the piano onstage and prepared to resume his final concert piece as the audience, still murmuring about all the excitement, settled back to enjoy the rest of the evening.

"Max, you wonder," Sylvia whispered, lifting Maximilian up on to Minette's table by the side of the stage. "You found the cats! I don't suppose you will ever be able to tell us how."

Oscar leapt up on to the table and slipped the medal from round his neck into Sylvia's hand.

"What's this, puss?" she asked, gazing at it.

"It's a choral medal," Minette said, taking it and turning it over in her hand. "I had one when I sang with the choir of St Bernice's." She held it up to the light.

"It's from Notre-Dame," she said, pointing to an inscription on the reverse of the medal.

"Is that where the cats were?" mused Sylvia. Both Maximilian and Oscar miaowed in agreement, and Sylvia took the medal and slipped it into her beaded evening bag. "We'll give this to Madame Emerald directly after the concert finishes," she said. "And we'll tell the police to search the cathedral." She gazed at Maximilian and Oscar. "You two are amazing, you really are."

The evening sped on. Henri finished his piece to tumultuous applause and there was a pause while the judges deliberated. Then Minette's name was called. She looked at the music in her hand, her face downcast. She had chosen another song from her repertoire, but Maximilian could see that she was not happy with it.

"It's nowhere near as lovely as the one that I was going to sing," she sighed. "But Julienne has sung that already."

Sylvia and Agnes exchanged looks, not sure what to say to cheer Minette up. Maximilian's whiskers tingled. He had had an idea, but how on earth was he to let Sylvia and Agnes know what it was? He glanced at Oscar, hoping that his friend would not laugh at him, then gave a cough to clear his throat and started to miaow the tune of the song that Minette had sung in the café.

"What on *earth* are you making that awful racket for, Max?" Sylvia cried. "Shh. They'll hear you on stage."

Maximilian frowned at her, but carried on miaowing, hoping that they would catch on to what he was trying to do before he had to miaow the very high notes that he knew were quite out of his range. His face was an agony of embarrassment as he yowled up the scale.

"Hang on," Minette said. "He's singing!"

"I wouldn't call it that," Agnes retorted, sticking her fingers in her ears.

"You're right," Sylvia said, listening a little more carefully. "It's that song you sang in the café. Oh!"

The three girls looked at one another.

"It might work," said Minette dubiously.

"It would be *perfect*!" Sylvia urged. "Just think how much everyone loved it, and you sang it beautifully."

Minette looked again at the music in her hand and made a decision. She cast it on to the table and strode out on to the stage to the pianist. She leaned down to whisper in his ear.

And then she sang.

Minette's voice rang out like silver on crystal, pure and clear in the silence of the hall. The audience held its breath. They had sat through a week of the most beautiful music written by the most celebrated composers in Europe. They had been delighted by full orchestras and by the skill of the pianist who now sat motionless by the silent grand piano on the stage. Here, on the last night of the competition, they were coaxed into breathless silence by the simplicity of Minette's voice singing a pure song of love.

Minette's song wove its spell around the room. Elderly men pressed the hands of their wives or whisked away tears. Young couples smiled fondly at one another. The judges laid down their pens.

Minette's final note rang out and the audience sighed.

Then they rose to their feet and the spell broke in a shower of applause as the room crowned its "Voice of Paris".

CHAPTER 20
The Most Beautiful City

"You were *perfect!*" gushed Sylvia.

"Just wonderful!" added Agnes.

"A well-deserved win," miaowed Maximilian and Oscar together.

They were back at the little café bar, *Theo's*. Madame Belfourte had suggested that they celebrate Minette's win at one of the more fashionable restaurants, but Madame Emerald had insisted that Minette choose her favourite place. Three small tables had been crammed together and round them sat Maximilian and his friends. The café bar buzzed with life and delicious-smelling dishes were whisked into sight in front of them. Maximilian was next to Eloise, suddenly finding himself very lost for words. Oscar and Peppi were bent over the menu, with Peppi pointing out all his favourite dishes. The two of them were most definitely *not* looking in the direction of Maximilian and Eloise.

Maximilian could not understand why he could not think of anything to say. It was as if he had forgotten every word he had ever known just when he needed them most. He was clearing his throat and trying to think of something clever when the café door sprang open and Monsieur Lavroche hurried over to join them.

"It's just as you thought, Sylvia," he said, shaking his coat out over the back of a chair. "A dozen cat baskets crammed up in the tower of Notre-Dame. The police are looking for fingerprints as we speak."

Agnes clapped her hands.

"Oh, clever, clever puss!" she cried, fussing over Oscar. "It was ingenious of you to steal that medal. We would never have guessed where the cats had been hidden without that."

"It was clever of Max too," Sylvia said, frowning a little. "He led all the cats to safety, remember."

"I think they work as a pair, these two," said Madame Emerald. She looked over at Peppi.

"I wonder if Monsieur Peppi helped at all."

Maximilian and Oscar miaowed their "of course he did, and Eloise helped too" miaows, but the humans had moved on to talk about the generous scholarship that Minette had been granted to study music at a conservatoire chosen by Madame Emerald. The four friends were left to talk among themselves.

"It has been a great adventure, Messieurs," said Peppi. "I will miss you both greatly."

"We could not have done it without your help," said Oscar. "Both of you were so courageous."

Maximilian nodded and silently wished that he had said this. Maximilian always considered himself to be an elegant sort of cat, but it was Oscar who always knew what to say, and Oscar who was able to put people at ease. Kindness, Maximilian supposed, was a special sort of elegance. Oscar really was a wonderful cat and remembering that such a cat was his friend gave Maximilian a little courage.

"Offering to be kidnapped by Zelie was very brave," he said. "I am very proud to have met you both."

Eloise smiled. "And I you," she said. "I hope—"

But they would never know what it was that Eloise hoped. With a little miaow of alarm she was whisked into the air by a tall man in a butler's uniform while Monsieur Lavroche helped her elderly mistress into a velvet evening coat.

"Don't forget me, my dear new friends," Eloise cried. She reached out for Maximilian and pressed something into his paw. He kept his eyes on her as she was carried out of the café. She lifted her paw to her mouth at the door to blow a kiss, and then she was gone.

Maximilian sighed. He did not think that he would ever meet another cat like her. He opened his paw to see what it was that Eloise had passed to him and his heart gave a little leap.

It was a twinkling diamond "E".

"A song from Minette!" cried a voice at the back of the café. "A song before she is too famous to sing for us!"

"I will *never* stop wanting to sing for you," Minette laughed, and she was swept away to the piano by a team of waiters in long aprons. Music was hastily arranged, a waiter tapped a crystal glass to signal for silence, and Minette's sweet voice rose again to delight a room full of people who had loved her for years and were happy for her.

Maximilian looked at the sparkling "E" lying in his paw. He would miss Eloise. He would miss Peppi too, and Minette, and even Madame Belfourte.

"Back to London tomorrow," said Oscar, as if reading his mind.

Maximilian nodded. Back to the theatre, and a new production for Sylvia and Agnes and perhaps a new adventure for himself and Oscar. He looked up at Peppi.

"But a little piece of us will always be in Paris," he said gallantly.

The humans had stood up, swaying to the beautiful sound of Minette's song. Some of them murmured softly along to it or gently clapped their hands in time with the rhythm.

"Remember us when you have your next adventure," said Peppi.

"Remember us when next you step out on the rooftops of Paris," said Maximilian.

The three cats raised a paw to one another.

Oscar and Peppi went back to their salmon soufflés. Maximilian sat for a while, listening to Minette's lovely voice and thinking about all that had happened over the last week. He had rescued a dozen cats. He had met still more brave ones. He had ridden in a hot air balloon and listened to beautiful music in elegant concert halls and tiny cafés. But the main thing that Maximilian thought, as Madame Emerald cheered for Minette's success and Sylvia and Agnes hugged one another in happiness for her, and Oscar and Peppi rattled their paws on the table in appreciation, was how lucky he was to have friends. At that moment Maximilian felt like the luckiest cat alive, and in his mind he raised a glass of the finest champagne to all those he loved, as the music played on and the laughter flowed in a tiny café in the most beautiful city in the world.

BOUQUETS

Dressing rooms like Madame Emerald's are often full of bouquets of flowers from friends and family and it's not unusual for the chorus to fill the chorus-room sink with flowers when they run out of vases for them. It's a lovely way to celebrate all the hard work that goes into a show. So here are the bouquets that I want to give out to the amazing people who helped bring Max and Oscar's Parisian adventure to you.

Roses-a-plenty for the Nosy Crow Team. For Kirsty Stansfield, Fiona Scoble and Lauren Fairgrieve, Max's wonderful editors – thank you for all your help and guidance and for always helping me iron out plot points and keep going till I have found "just" the right word. Especial thanks to Fiona for correcting all my French. For Elisabetta Barbazza, Ray Tierney and Nicola Theobald – thank you for always making the books look so beautiful. For Ola Gotkowska and all the rights team – thank you for championing Max around the world. Seeing his adventures in so many languages has been an utter delight.

Buckets of blooms for Joanna Moult, the best agent in the world. Thank you for believing in Max and me from the outset and for every encouraging note and phone call that makes me feel like there is no problem I cannot solve.

Huge bouquets for the incredibly talented Nicola Kinnear. How on earth can I ever praise your illustrations enough? Max and Oscar leap off the page and I am so grateful that I get to work with you.

Beautiful blossoms for all the booksellers, book bloggers and teachers who have read Max and shared him with new readers. A special tail-whisk from Max to all the lovely readers who have sent me such lovely post. I love each and every letter.

Red and white roses for my lovely Yorkshire and Lancashire family, and Welsh daffodils for Seren – this book is for you, our own Winter Star. You are wonderful and I am so proud of you.

Perfect posies for my gorgeous Prime Writers, all my Twitter friends, my lovely work colleagues for celebrating each step, and my theatre friends for reminding me why I wanted to write about the theatre in the first place. Also Debbie and Cat for being awesome friends.

All the roses in the world for Neil, for always believing in me, making me smile when I really need it and putting up with me taking endless photos of Paris.

Finally, the most unusual bouquet of them all – a bundle of catnip for every cat I grew up with, many of whom have found their way into this book. Thank you for the purrs, the cuddles and for showing me how amazing cats are. I hope I captured your wonderful personalities well.

Sarah xxxx